The Pocket Guide

to

Rituals

MAGICKAL REFERENCES AT YOUR FINGERTIPS

KERRI CONNOR

A division of The Career Press
Franklin Lakes, NJ

THE POCKET GUIDE TO RITUALS
Cover design by Digi Dog Design NYC
Printed in the U.S.A. by Book-mart Press
Interior Illustrations by Colleen Koziara, Mystical Willow
Productions (*www.mysticalwillow.com*)

To order this title, please call toll-free 1-800-CAREER-1 (NJ and Canada: 201-848-0310) to order using VISA or MasterCard, or for further information on books from Career Press.

The Career Press, Inc., 3 Tice Road, PO Box 687,
Franklin Lakes, NJ 07417
www.careerpress.com
www.newpagebooks.com

Library of Congress Cataloging-in-Publication Data

Available upon request.

DEDICATION

This book goes out to all of my sisters,

with an extra special thank you

to Carrie.

∽

Contents

Rituals of Nature

Introduction

Many Pagans celebrate the eight festivals of the Wheel of the Year with rituals to commemorate these special holidays in a Pagan's life, but there are many other events in the life of a Pagan that also deserve special rituals to honor these occasions.

Some of the rituals in this book are common to most Pagans, but others you may never have thought of before. Some are more for fun, while others are of a more serious nature. Either way, this book is designed to help you easily and effectively create rituals for these particular events.

Why do we celebrate with ritual? Each person may be able to answer this question differently, but, to me, there are four distinct reasons:

1. **Focused attention and energy.** Rituals give us a chance to focus our attention and energy on a particular subject or event. Channeling this attention and energy into the ritual has the benefit of transferring positive energy to another person or into an object. Positive events in our lives

deserve positive attention. We often worry so much about the negative; it's time the good in life is given center stage.

2. **Spiritual expression.** Any time we perform a ritual we are spiritually expressing ourselves. The more we express ourselves spiritually, the easier it becomes to know when and how to do so.

3. **Show of thankfulness.** As human beings, we often complain when things just aren't going right in our lives. We should be able to express the joy and thankfulness in our lives, just as easily (if not more so!) than we do the negative. As a society, we are not always encouraged to celebrate the good in life—the world is filled with negative attention. We need to celebrate the positive more and be thankful for what it is we *do* have!

4. **Communion with others.** Everybody loves a good party, and a good ritual generally turns into one! As human beings, we need connections with other people (and animals too!). They help to keep us happy and emotionally healthy. Share your rituals with those you love!

How to Use This Book

This book is divided into two sections: Rituals of Life and Rituals of Nature.

Rituals of Life include life's milestones from birth to death along with special events such as getting a job or new home. These events will come to different people at different times in their lives, but everyone can and should celebrate them when they happen.

Rituals of Nature include different events that happen in nature, some on a daily basis (such as Sunrise and Sunset) and some on an annual basis (Changing of the Leaves or First Snow). Other Rituals of Nature, such as Celebration of Air, can be performed whenever you feel them to be most appropriate or when you really feel you need the connection the ritual is designed to create.

Although we have Sabbats that celebrate events such as the beginning of Spring or Summer, depending on where you live, these rituals may feel more symbolic than what the weather is telling us. For example, a year ago, our Beltaine in northern Illinois was sunny and in the 70s. This year it was in the 40s and we dodged thunderstorms. Sometimes the season being celebrated may not feel quite "right."

This book will make it easy for you to plan your rituals by listing different ritual elements from which to choose. There are several categories of components listed for each ritual type. These include: theme, colors, crystals and stones, altar decorations and incense, oils, and herbs.

To begin, you will look through the list of themes and pick which aspects on which you want your ritual to focus. Then, go through each additional category, choosing items that support your theme and that will be easy for you to obtain. It is that easy. Because many of the listed items have several different energies associated with them, only their qualities that relate to the given themes will be listed.

Appendixes A and B provide information on how to help you write the words for your own rituals, along with a template to keep track of the rituals you perform. I highly recommend putting together some kind of book in which to keep track of your rituals.

Creating your own rituals can be confusing and difficult. *The Pocket Guide to Rituals* is here to help you along every step of the way, making the process easy and enjoyable—just the way it should be!

PART ONE

Rituals of Life

1

Birth

Themes

Choose two or three themes on which to center your ritual.

- Celebrating life cycles
- Comfort
- Consecration
- Good health
- Growth
- Happiness
- Happy home
- Hope
- Love
- Luck
- New beginnings
- Patience (both for the baby and for the new parents)
- Peace
- Peaceful sleep
- Protection
- Security
- Strength
- Well-being

Colors

Choose colors that support your theme.

Black: absorbing negative energy and protection
Blue: hope, peaceful sleep, and protection
Brown: strength
Gold: strength, the Gods, and masculinity (good for male babies)
Green: growth, good health, luck, comfort, and security
Light blue: calmness, patience, and good health
Pink: love, household peace, and comfort
Purple: growth and strength
Red: strength and life cycles
Silver: femininity and the goddesses (good for baby girls)
Violet: peaceful sleep and healing
White: consecrating, peace, protection, innocence, and good health
Yellow: happiness

Crystals and Stones

Choose crystals and stones that support your theme.

Calming, good health, strength, and aids restful sleep: hematite
Good health: smokey quartz
Good health and comfort: sodalite
Good health and protection: jasper
Good health, comfort, and aids growth: celestite
Good health, protection, love, and peace: jade
Happiness: ruby
Happiness, love, protection, and good health: lapis lazuli
Joy and happiness: amazonite

Love, peace, happiness, and good health: rose quartz
Love, peaceful sleep, protection, and peace: moonstone
      and tourmaline
Luck: opal
Luck, happiness, protection, and good health: chrysoprase
Luck, love, and happiness: alexandrite
Luck, peace, and good health: aventurine
Peace: aquamarine, carnelian, and rhodonite
Peace and calming: calcite and kunzite
Peace and love: chrysocalla and emerald
Peace, happiness, and love: amethyst
Peace, luck, and protection: lepidolite
Protection: citrine, obsidian, and sunstone
Protection and luck: tiger's-eye
Protection and strength: onyx
Protection, good health, love, and comfort: topaz
Protection, love, and good health: zircon
Protection, love, and peace: malachite
Protection, luck, good health, and happiness: turquoise
Protection, sleep, and good health: peridot
Strength: bloodstone
Strength, good health, and protection: diamond and garnet
Strength, love, and protection: agate

Incense, Oils, and Herbs

Choose incense, oils, and herbs that support your theme.

Good health and protection: anemone, bittersweet, and
      blackberry
Good health, love, and protection: geranium and ginseng

Love, good health, and protection: beryl and sapphire

Good health, peace, and protection: olive

Happiness: witch grass

Healing and protection: rowan

Health: sassafras and sunflower

Health and love: rue

Health and protection: yerba santa

Health, protection, strength, love, and happiness: St. John's wort

Love: apricot, aster, bachelor's buttons, bleeding heart, lady's mantle, orchid, rye, sarsaparilla, senna, spearmint, spikenard, strawberry, sugar cane, tamarind, vetivert, and yarrow

Love and good health: apple and coriander

Love and happiness: Adam and Eve root

Love and luck: daffodil

Love and peace: scullcap

Love and protection: basil, clover, dragon's blood, parsley, primrose, and willow

Love, healing, happiness, and strength: saffron

Love, healing, luck, and protection: rose

Love, peace, and happiness: meadowsweet

Love, peace, and healing: gardenia

Love, peaceful sleep, and protection: valerian

Love, protection, and good health: balm of Gilead and barley

Love, protection, and happiness: hyacinth

Love, protection, sleep, happiness, and peace: lavender

Love, sleep, and luck: poppy

Luck: bluebell

Luck and healing: allspice

Protection: African violet, chrysanthemum, feverfew, frankincense, sage, snapdragon, Solomon's seal, witch hazel, and woodruff

Protection and good health: angelica, burdock, cedar, eucalyptus, and fennel

Protection and happiness: cyclamen

Protection and healing: sandalwood

Protection and love: wormwood

Protection and luck: aloe, bamboo, dill, and heather

Protection and restful sleep: agrimony

Protection, good health, and strength: bay and carnation

Protection, healing, and luck: oak

Protection, love, and health: mandrake

Protection, love, and peace: violet

Protection, love, good health, and sleep: rosemary

Protection, love, happiness, and good health: marjoram

Restful sleep, health, and love: thyme

Sleep, love, and purification: chamomile

Strength: sweetpea

Strength and protection: mugwort and thistle

Strength, protection, and peace: pennyroyal

Altar Decorations

There are dozens of ideas you can use to decorate your altar for a ritual celebrating the birth of a new life. Try using a receiving blanket for an altar cloth. Use items that represent your baby, including baby's first picture, toys, a rattle, baby shoes or booties, a bottle or a pacifier. You may also want to include pictures of family members who have already passed on. In your ritual, you can ask these ancestors to help protect and look over your child.

When choosing your colors, you may want to include the "traditional" pink for girls or blue for boys, or you can add in silver for femininity and the goddesses, or gold for masculinity and the gods.

Go over your list of themes and pick out items that can symbolize those qualities. Maybe you keep a four leaf clover, which would work well for luck. Comfort could be symbolized by a soft, warm blanket. Love can always be shown in the image of a heart. You can cut small hearts out of paper in your corresponding colors and sprinkle them all over your altar. The ancient Chinese *kang* is a symbol of good health. The dove has been used by many religions for centuries to symbolize peace.

Incorporate the colors you have chosen with flowers, ribbons, and candles.

Make a fresh bouquet of your chosen herbs and flowers. Crush dried herbs and flowers into incense and burn on a charcoal tab. Pure oils can be dripped onto a lit charcoal tab to release a burst of scent in a beautiful cloud.

Ceremony

Begin your ritual as you normally would with your own version of creating a circle and calling the quarters. Once you have completed your normal ritual opening, you may proceed using this sample ritual. You will also use your own closing once you have completed the specific ritual.

The baby should be present, but take care to keep the baby out of the direct flow of the incense smoke.

Say the following:

Oh great Lord and Lady, Father and Mother of us all, we come to you today to ask for your blessings upon this child, son/daughter of (mother's name) and (father's name).

As we celebrate this birth in the spiral of life, we ask you to bless (baby's name) with peace and take him/her under your protective wing.

May your love and light forever shine down upon (baby's name). May he/she grow to know your love, strength, and power in his/her own time, as well as the love, strength, and power that resides within her/his own heart.

May peace forever surround this child, but when difficulties arise, may (baby's name) have the strength to see them through.

As the wheel keeps turning, we shall rejoice in this gift of life, and celebrate each milestone (baby's name) achieves.

Thank you, Lord and Lady, for bestowing your blessings and love upon this child.

2

Menarche/Puberty

Themes

Choose two or three themes on which to center you ritual.

- Celebrating life cycles
- Courage
- Femininity
- Fertility
- Growth
- Happiness
- Hope
- Love
- Masculinity
- Moon (for females)
- New beginnings
- Patience
- Protection
- Strength
- Sun (for males)

Colors

Choose colors that support your theme.

Black: protection
Blue: protection, hope, and change

Brown: strength
Gold: the God, strength, courage, and masculinity
Green: growth and fertility
Indigo: change
Light blue: patience
Magenta: change
Orange: courage
Pink: love
Purple: growth and inner strength
Red: courage, strength, blood, and life cycle
Silver: the Goddess, moon power, and femininity
White: protection
Yellow: happiness and sun power

Crystals and Stones

Choose crystals and stones that support your theme.

Courage: aquamarine and carnelian
Courage and happiness: ruby
Courage and protection: tiger's-eye
Courage and strength: bloodstone
Courage, happiness, and love: amethyst
Courage, happiness, love, and protection: lapis lazuli
Courage, protection, and happiness: turquoise
Courage, strength, and protection: diamond
Courage, strength, love, and protection: agate
Growth: celestite
Happiness: amazonite
Happiness and protection: chrysoprase
Love: alexandrite, chrysocolla, emerald, and rhodochrosite

Love and happiness: rose quartz
Love and protection: beryl, sapphire, and zircon
Love, courage, and protection: tourmaline
Protection: citrine, jasper, obsidian, peridot, and sunstone
Protection and love: malachite, moonstone, and topaz
Protection, love, fertility, and courage: jade
Strength and protection: garnet, lepidolite, and onyx

Incense, Oils, and Herbs

Choose incense, oils, and herbs that support your theme.

Courage: borage
Courage and love: columbine and yarrow
Courage, protection, and love: mullein
Fertility: bistort and carrot
Fertility and happiness: hawthorn
Fertility and love: chickweed, daffodil, and fig
Fertility and protection: bodhi, mustard, oak, olive, pine, and rice
Fertility, love, and protection: geranium
Fertility, protection, and happiness: cyclamen
Love: apple, bachelor's buttons, and bleeding heart (very symbolic for a female's ritual)
Love and happiness: Adam and Eve root, catnip, and witch grass
Love and protection: balm of Gilead, barley, basil, bloodroot (very symbolic for a female's ritual), parsley, and violet
Love, courage, and protection: cohosh
Love, protection, and happiness: hyacinth and marjoram
Protection: African violet, agrimony, aloe, alyssum, amaranth, anemone, and angelica
Protection and happiness: celandine

Protection and love: clove and dragon's blood
Protection and spirituality: myrrh (for use with God or Goddess
      themes)
Protection and strength: bay and carnation
Protection, love, and fertility: mandrake
Protection, strength, love, and happiness: St. John's wort
Spirituality and protection: frankincense
Strength and protection: mugwort

Altar Decorations

Decorations for this altar should be representative of a young adult. Include items that symbolize the themes you have chosen. If you are including fertility in your theme, you can include a rabbit (real or fake), or something from a garden such as corn. Growth can be symbolized with a live plant. The Japanese symbol *Nintai* represents patience.

An interesting item to include in rituals that celebrate life cycles is anything with a spiral form to it. You can make paper spirals by cutting a round piece of paper and then continue to cut following the edge all the way around, continually turning the circle until you reach the center. If your ritual is indoors, you can hang these spirals from the ceiling. If you are outside, hang these from trees or staked poles stuck in the ground. You can also stretch out metal springs for the same effect.

If your ritual is for a female, you should include plenty of red and silver, and lunar symbols. Decorate the altar and area around it with red and silver glitter or confetti. If outdoors, hang red and silver ribbons from tree branches if they are available.

You can often find wooden moon cutouts at your local craft store. Paint them and hang them around your altar and circle area. Cut out small shapes of different moon phases from white or metallic silver piece of paper and scatter them on your altar. Larger moon shapes can also be hung.

If your ritual is for a male, you may wish to emphasize masculinity with the color gold. He will most likely want to relate more with the God now as he defines himself as a man. Incorporate sun images into your decorations. Cut out sun shapes and hang them, or find sun shapes from a craft store and paint them. You can probably find sun-shaped confetti at a party supply store.

Incorporate the colors you have chosen with flowers, ribbons, and candles.

Make a fresh bouquet of your chosen herbs and flowers. Use dried herbs and flowers to crush into incense to burn on a charcoal tab. Pure oils can be dripped onto a lit charcoal tab to release a burst of scent in a beautiful cloud.

Ceremony

Begin your ritual as you normally would with your own version of creating a circle and calling the quarters. Once you have completed your normal ritual opening you may proceed using this sample ritual. You will also use your own closing once you have completed the specific ritual.

Say the following:

(Bring the female the ritual is for to the center of the circle near the altar.)

Lady of the Moon, we come to you this night to honor (female's name) as she passes from the life of a child to the life of a maiden.

As the spiral of life continues, we all take on different forms.

Maiden, Mother, Crone. Maiden, Mother, Crone.

(Female's name) now begins her journey to follow in the footsteps of the women that have come before her.

Maiden, Mother, Crone. Maiden, Mother, Crone.

As (female's name) grows and learns, we ask that you look over and protect her.

Maiden, Mother, Crone. Maiden, Mother, Crone.

Through your love, and ours, she will learn of the Mysteries of womanhood.

Maiden, Mother, Crone. Maiden, Mother, Crone.

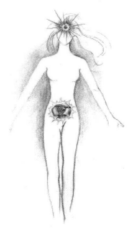

As daughters of the Great Mother, we are all sisters in
love.

Maiden, Mother, Crone. Maiden, Mother, Crone.

(Bring out triple Goddess necklace and pass through the smoke of the ground frankincense and myrrh while saying the next few lines.)

We ask for your blessing upon this gift, this symbol of
your love and our love for (female's name).

Maiden, Mother, Crone. Maiden, Mother, Crone.

(Put necklace around female's neck)

May she always find comfort and strength in your open
arms.

(At this point each woman may give the female a gift or relate a personal story about her growth to a maiden. When all our finished continue.)

As daughters of the Great Mother, we are all sisters in
love.

Maiden, Mother, Crone. Maiden, Mother, Crone,

3

Birthdays

Themes

Choose two or three themes on which to center your ritual.

- ∾ Celebrating life cycles
- ∾ Growth
- ∾ Happiness
- ∾ Health
- ∾ Love
- ∾ Prosperity
- ∾ Protection
- ∾ Success
- ∾ Wisdom

Colors

Choose colors that support your theme.

Black: protection
Blue: protection, change, and wisdom
Green: growth and prosperity
Indigo: change
Magenta: change

Pink: love and success
Purple: growth and success
Red: life cycle
White: protection
Yellow: happiness

Crystals and Stones

Choose crystals and stones that support your theme.

Aids growth: celestite
Happiness and love: amethyst
Happiness and protection: chrysoprase
Love: chrysocolla and rhodochrosite
Love and happiness: rose quartz
Love and joy: alexandrite
Love and protection: agate, beryl, malachite, moonstone, and zircon
Love, happiness, protection, and prosperity: lapis lazuli
Love, prosperity, and protection: sapphire and topaz
Prosperity and happiness: ruby
Prosperity and love: emerald
Protection: citrine, diamond, garnet, jasper, lepidolite, obsidian, onyx, and sunstone
Protection and prosperity: peridot, tiger's-eye, and tourmaline
Protection, wisdom, and prosperity: jade
Success and happiness: amazonite

Incense, Oils, and Herbs

Choose incense, oils, and herbs that support your theme.

Happiness: lily of the valley and witch grass

Love: apple, apricot, bachelor's buttons, and bleeding heart
Love and happiness: Adam and Eve root, catnip, and meadowsweet
Love and protection: balm of Gilead, barley, basil, bloodroot, clover, dragon's blood, ginseng, mimosa, mint, mistletoe, rose, willow, wormwood
Love and success: ginger
Love, protection, and happiness: hyacinth, lavender, marjoram, and St. John's wort
Love, success, and happiness: High John the Conquerer
Prosperity: alfalfa and banana
Prosperity and love: nuts
Prosperity and wisdom: almond
Protection: aloe, alyssum, anemone, angelica, bamboo, bittersweet, broom, buckthorn, honeysuckle, hyssop, Irish moss, and lady's slipper
Protection and happiness: cyclamen
Protection and prosperity: elder
Protection and strength: bay
Protection and success: rowan
Success and love: Cinnamon

Altar Decorations

Birthday rituals should be fun, so feel free to use party decorations, such as streamers, to decorate your altar and ritual area. Your decorations will need to be suited to the age of the birthday person, of course, but have some fun with it.

Look through your choices of themes and find objects and ideas that symbolize those blessings you want to bestow upon the birthday person. The Japanese *kenkou* is the symbol for health.

This kind of symbol can be painted on rocks or a small piece of wood and placed on the altar. You can also paint the names of other themes on rocks and place them throughout the ritual area.

Most party supply stores will have a large assortment of smiley face items, which will work perfectly for happiness.

Incorporate the colors you have chosen with flowers, ribbons, and candles.

Make a fresh bouquet of your chosen herbs and flowers. Crush dried herbs and flowers into incense and burn on a charcoal tab. Pure oils can be dripped onto a lit charcoal tab to release a burst of scent in a beautiful cloud.

Ceremony

Begin your ritual as you normally would with your own version of creating a circle and calling the quarters. Once you have completed your normal ritual opening you may proceed using this sample ritual. You will also use your own closing once you have completed the specific ritual.

Say the following:

Lord and Lady, we call upon you this night to join together with us and celebrate this rite. The birthday of (person's name) is our reason to rejoice. We call out in celebration together as one voice. These candles burn for blessings we wish to be bestowed upon the very one of us who is another year old! Blessings of prosperity, and happiness too, are the gifts we've come to ask for our friend from You. Love and light, light and love. Blessings for our friend. Thank you, Lord and Lady, for the blessings that you send.

4

Adulthood

Themes

Choose two or three themes on which to center your ritual.

- ல் Celebrating life cycles
- ல் Growth
- ல் Happiness
- ல் Health
- ல் Love
- ல் Prosperity
- ல் Protection
- ல் Success
- ல் Wisdom

Colors

Choose colors that support your theme.

Black: protection
Blue: protection, change, and wisdom
Green: growth and prosperity
Indigo: change
Magenta: change
Pink: love and success

Purple: growth and success
Red: life cycle
White: protection
Yellow: happiness

Crystals and Stones

Choose crystals and stones that support your theme.

Aids growth: celestite
Happiness and love: amethyst
Happiness and protection: chrysoprase
Love: chrysocolla and rhodochrosite
Love and happiness: rose quartz
Love and joy: alexandrite
Love and protection: agate, beryl, and zircon
Love, happiness, protection, and prosperity: lapis lazuli
Love, prosperity, and protection: sapphire and topaz
Prosperity and happiness: ruby
Prosperity and love: emerald
Protection: citrine, diamond, garnet, jasper, lepidolite, obsidian, onyx, and sunstone
Protection and love: malachite and moonstone
Protection and prosperity: peridot, tiger's-eye, and tourmaline
Protection, wisdom, and prosperity: jade
Success and happiness: amazonite

Incense, Oils, and Herbs

Choose incense, oils, and herbs that support your theme.

Happiness: lily of the valley and witch grass

Love and happiness: Adam and Eve root, catnip, and meadowsweet

Love and protection: balm of Gilead, barley, basil, bloodroot, clover, dragon's blood, ginseng, mimosa, mint, mistletoe, rose, willow, and wormwood

Love, protection, and happiness: hyacinth, lavender, marjoram, and St. John's wort

Love, success, and happiness: High John the Conqueror

Love: apple, apricot, bachelor's buttons, and bleeding heart

Prosperity and love: nuts

Prosperity and wisdom: almond

Prosperity: alfalfa and banana

Protection and happiness: cyclamen

Protection and prosperity: elder

Protection and success: rowan

Protection: aloe, alyssum, anemone, angelica, bamboo, bay, bittersweet, broom, buckthorn, honeysuckle, hyssop, Irish moss, and lady's slipper

Success and love: cinnamon and ginger

Altar Decorations

Different people have different ideas of when adulthood occurs. Some say it's at age 18, others say age 21, and still others say it depends on the maturity level of the individual in question. Whichever way you look at adulthood, it can be a momentous occasion for the person beginning to experience it.

You may want to celebrate this occasion by saying "goodbye" to items from childhood and "hello" to items from adulthood. Setting up an altar in this manner opens a world of possibilities for decorations you can use. Bring out items from the person's childhood, such as toys, books, games, stuffed animals, blankets, or other keepsake mementos. These can be placed on one side of the altar with wishes for the future on the other side. Symbols can be used to represent these wishes—a miniature house or car represent a house or car in the person's future.

You can also use symbols to represent other aspects of your theme.

Incorporate the colors you have chosen with flowers, ribbons, and candles.

Make a fresh bouquet of your chosen herbs and flowers. Crush dried herbs and flowers and use as incense to burn on a charcoal tab. Pure oils can be dripped onto a lit charcoal tab to release a burst of scent in a beautiful cloud.

Ceremony

Begin your ritual as you normally would with your own version of creating a circle and calling the quarters. Once you have completed your normal ritual opening you may proceed using this sample ritual. You will also use your own closing once you have completed the specific ritual.

Say the following:

Today we come together to send (person's name) on a road of well wishes. A road which began the day (name) was born. A road that has taken many twists and turns, and will take many more in the years to come.

Sometimes the road will be bumpy, and sometimes the road will be smooth, but no matter where your journey takes you, the Lord and Lady will be right with you.

With this new journey, (name) takes on many new responsibilities. Responsibilities to herself/himself, and to those he/she loves. On this new journey, (name) will need strength and maturity, for him/her to thrive.

We come to you, Lord and Lady, to ask for blessings upon him/her. We ask for the blessing of prosperity. Lord and Lady, Lady and Lord. We ask for the blessing of success. Lord and Lady, Lady and Lord. We ask for the blessing of wisdom. Lord and Lady, Lady and Lord. We ask for the blessing of love. Lord and Lady, Lady and Lord.

As (name) travels the road of adulthood, our love and blessings go with him/her.

5

Paganing

Generally, when you see the word *Paganing*, you may think of a ritual where a baby is brought before the altar and the gods and goddesses are asked to protect and bless the child. However, because it is also generally a Pagan practice to allow each person to choose his or her own path, to me it has always seemed slightly at odds with this definition of a Paganing.

Because of my own feelings on this matter, my definition of a Paganing is a ritual for an adult who has decided to follow a Pagan path. This is different than a dedication to a certain path. Most likely, many of us realized we were Pagan before finding a specific path that felt right to us. Over the years, many Pagans have also traded the paths they were on for a different one. This ritual, therefore, is simply a declaration, a statement that one has decided to find and follow a Pagan path, even if that specific path has not yet shown itself.

Themes

Choose two or three themes on which to center your ritual.

- Celebrating life cycles
- The Elements
- Happiness
- Honor
- The God
- The Goddess
- Love
- Protection
- Purification
- Spirituality
- Wisdom

Colors

Choose colors that support your theme.

Black: protection
Blue: protection, honor, change, virgin goddesses, wisdom, and knowledge
Brown: earth
Gold: the Gods and solar deities
Indigo: insight and change
Magenta: intuition and change
Pink: love and honor
Purple: insight, inspiration, and spirituality
Red: life cycle
Silver: the Goddesses, intuition, and lunar deities
Turquoise: honor
Violet: intuition and spiritual awareness
White: protection and purification

Colors for the Elements

Earth: black, brown, green, and gold
Air: white, lavender, and pale blue
Water: blue, blue-green, aquamarine, indigo, and white
Fire: red, orange, yellow, and gold

Crystals and Stones

Choose crystals and stones that support your theme.

Happiness and love: amethyst
Happiness and protection: chrysoprase
Intuition: hematite
Joy: amazonite
Love: emerald and rhodochrosite
Love and happiness: rose quartz
Love, spiritual transformation, and joy: alexandrite
Protection: citrine, jasper, obsidian, onyx, sunstone, tiger's-eye, and turquoise
Protection and intuition: peridot
Protection and love: agate, beryl, jade, lapis lazuli, malachite, moonstone, sapphire, topaz, tourmaline, and zircon
Protection and purification: garnet
Protection and spirituality: diamond
Purification: aquamarine and calcite
Spirituality and protection: lepidolite
Wisdom: chrysocolla and sodalite

Incense, Oils, and Herbs

Choose incense, oils, and herbs that support your theme.

Love: apple, aster, bachelor's button, bleeding heart, chickweed, coltsfoot, columbine, and ginger

Love and happiness: Adam and Eve root and catnip

Love and protection: balm of Gilead, barley, basil, clover, dragon's blood, elecampane, ginseng, and mandrake

Love and purification: copal

Love and spirituality: gardenia

Love, protection, and happiness: hyacinth and marjoram

Love, protection, and purification: bloodroot, parsley, and vervain

Love, protection, purification, and happiness: lavender

Protection and happiness: celandine and cyclamen

Protection and love: violet and wormwood

Protection and purification: bay, birch, broom, cedar, fennel, hyssop, valerian, and yucca

Protection and spirituality: frankincense, myrrh, and sandalwood

Protection: agrimony, aloe, alyssum, amaranth, anemone, angelica, bittersweet, bladderwrack, buckthorn, carnation, chrysanthemum, dill, eucalyptus, fern, feverfew, geranium, heather, holly, juniper, and lady's slipper

Purification: chamomile

Purification and love: lemon verbena and thyme

Spirituality: cinnamon

Spirituality and protection: African violet

Wisdom, protection, and purification: sage

Altar Decorations

This is a highly spiritual ritual and the decorations should reflect that. Include natural items to represent the elements. You may already have items on your altar that represent the elements, but for this type of ritual you may want to use more.

Include any statuary or pictures of the deities you may have. Remember this is a more serious ritual, but you can still have fun with it.

Incorporate the colors you have chosen with flowers, ribbons, and candles.

Make a fresh bouquet of your chosen herbs and flowers. Use dried herbs and flowers to crush into incense to burn on a charcoal tab. Pure oils can be dripped onto a lit charcoal tab to release a burst of scent in a beautiful cloud.

Ceremony

Begin your ritual as you normally would with your own version of creating a circle and calling the quarters. Once you have completed your normal ritual opening you may proceed using this sample ritual. You will also use your own closing once you have completed the specific ritual.

Say the following:

> *We call upon you, O great Goddess, Lady of light, Mother of Earth, and mother to us all, as (name) comes to you to ask for admittance into your loving arms, and to pledge his/her love and devotion.*

> *We call upon you, O Great Horned God, Lord of the woods, Father of all things wild, and Father to us all, as*

(name) comes to you to ask for admittance into your open arms, and to pledge his/her love and devotion.

Person the Paganing is for should say the following:

I pledge myself to honor thee, love thee, and serve thee, as I tread through life, searching for the path designed for my heart to follow.

I swear my oath, to learn, to study, to seek, to love, while on my quest to find the true names of my Lord, my Lady, and myself.

6

College

Themes

Choose two or three themes on which to center your ritual.

- ☙ Celebrating life cycles
- ☙ Mental powers
- ☙ Protection
- ☙ Stability
- ☙ Success
- ☙ Wisdom

Colors

Choose colors that support your theme.

Black: protection
Blue: protection, change, and wisdom
Brown: stability and concentration
Gold: success and confidence
Green: security
Indigo: change
Magenta: change
Orange: success and ambition

Pink: success
Purple: ambition
Red: life cycle
Silver: stability
Violet: success
White: protection
Yellow: intelligence, study, mind power, and examinations and
    tests

Crystals and Stones

Choose crystals and stones that support your theme.

Concentration: azurite
Emotional balance: opal
Mental abilities and balance: emerald and rhodochrosite
Mental agility: aventurine
Mental and emotional balance: moldavite
Mental clarity, memory, and confidence: rhodonite
Protection: agate, beryl, chrysoprase, diamond, garnet, jasper,
    lapis lazuli, lepidolite, malachite, moonstone, obsidian,
    sapphire, sunstone, tiger's-eye, and tourmaline
Protection and emotional balance: onyx, peridot, topaz, and
    turquoise
Protection and wisdom: jade
Protection, emotional balance, and mental alertness: zircon
Success: amazonite
Wisdom: chrysocolla and sodalite

Incense, Oils, and Herbs

Choose incense, oils, and herbs that support your theme.

Conscious mind: costmary, lavender, and saffron

Memory: clove and coriander

Memory and mental powers: honeysuckle

Mental alertness and protection: black pepper and horehound

Mental powers: celery seeds, fenugreek, rue, tangerine, and vanilla

Mental powers and the conscious mind: lily of the valley

Mental powers, protection, the conscious mind, and memory: rosemary

Mental stimulant: peppermint

Protection: African violet, agrimony, aloe, alyssum, amaranth, anemone, angelica, balm of Gilead, basil, bittersweet, and cumin

Protection and the conscious mind: dill, garlic, hyssop, pennyroyal, and petitgrain

Stability and self-confidence: amber

Success: woodruff

Wisdom: almond and sunflower

Wisdom, the conscious mind, and memory: sage

Altar Decorations

Whether you are attending a local school or going away to live somewhere else, beginning college is an exciting new adventure.

These days, college has become extremely important and necessary in order to get a well-paying job and start out on a chosen career. Although college can also be a lot of fun, it does have to be taken seriously to an extent. With the cost of tuition these days, it would be plain silly to thrown it away.

Your ritual should reflect this—serious, yet fun at the appropriate times.

Some altar decorations you can use would include text books, the college acceptance letter, even report cards from high school. Any items you have from the college can be used too, such as a mascot or pennant.

Use other symbols to represent your chosen themes.

Incorporate the colors you have chosen with flowers, ribbons, and candles.

Make a fresh bouquet of your chosen herbs and flowers. Use dried herbs and flowers to crush into incense to burn on a charcoal tab. Pure oils can be dripped onto a lit charcoal tab to release a burst of scent in a beautiful cloud.

Ceremony

Begin your ritual as you normally would with your own version of creating a circle and calling the quarters. Once you have completed your normal ritual opening you may proceed using this sample ritual. You will also use your own closing once you have completed the specific ritual.

Say the following:

Great God and Great Goddess, I come before you today to thank you for the opportunity put before me, and to ask for your blessings as I embark on this new adventure.

Knowledge and wisdom are the keys to life and success, and so I ask for your blessing of knowledge upon me. I ask for your blessing of wisdom upon me. I ask for your blessing of success upon me.

As I travel to (college's name), I ask for your protection to keep me safe. As I am away from my family, I ask for your protection and for your comfort to make me feel at home away from home.

Great God and Great Goddess, grant me the wisdom to make the right choices. Grant me the strength to follow through where I need. Grant me the love and compassion to help those who I can.

Great God and Great Goddess, these are the blessings I ask for in your name.

7

Engagement

Themes

Choose two or three themes on which to center your ritual.

- Abundance
- Affection
- Balance
- Communication
- Celebrating life cycles
- Endurance
- Energy
- Fertility
- Fidelity
- Friendship
- Growth
- Happiness
- Harmony
- Honesty
- Honor
- Love
- New beginnings
- Passion
- Patience
- Peace
- Prosperity
- Romance
- Security
- Sensuality
- Sex
- Stability
- Strength
- Tranquility
- Truth
- Understanding
- Unity
- Vitality

Colors

Choose colors that support your theme.

Blue: truth, tranquility, honor, peace, fidelity, and unity
Brown: stability, sensuality, endurance, strength, and grace
Gold: vitality and strength
Green: abundance, growth, prosperity, fertility, and security
Light blue: tranquility, patience, and understanding
Orange: enthusiasm, energy, friendship, and communication
Pink: compassion, tenderness, harmony, affection, love, romance,
and honor
Purple: growth
Red: sexual love, passion, energy, and strength
Silver: truth, stability, and balance
Turquoise: honor
White: peace, truth, and tranquility
Yellow: joy, vitality, and communication

Crystals and Stones

Choose crystals and stones that support your theme.

Balance: moldavite
Balance and strength: onyx
Communication, peace, and balance: kunzite
Compassion and growth: celestite
Energy: jasper
Energy and love: beryl
Energy, love, and peace: malachite
Energy, peace, love, and balance: rhodochrosite

Fertility: geode
Intensifies energy: clear quartz
Joy: amazonite
Joy, love, fidelity, and prosperity: lapis lazuli
Love and joy: alexandrite
Love, friendship, prosperity, peace, and energy: tourmaline
Love, harmony, and peace: moonstone
Love, peace, and happiness: rose quartz
Love, peace, and prosperity: sapphire
Love, peace, sexual energy, and balance: zircon
Passion and sexuality: sunstone
Peace: aquamarine, aventurine, calcite, and rhodonite
Peace and balance: lepidolite
Peace, happiness, and love: amethyst
Peace, love, communication, and vitality: chrysocolla
Prosperity and balance: opal peridot
Prosperity and joy: ruby
Prosperity, balance, love, and tranquility: topaz
Prosperity, energy, and honesty: tiger's-eye
Prosperity, friendship, communication, happiness, and balance: turquoise
Prosperity, happiness, and friendship: chrysoprase
Prosperity, love, fertility, and peace: jade
Prosperity, love, peace, and balance: emerald
Sexual energy: citrine
Sexual energy and peace: carnelian
Strength: bloodstone
Strength and love: agate
Strength and sexual abilities: diamond
Strength, energy, and compassion: garnet

Incense, Oils, and Herbs

Choose incense, oils, and herbs that support your theme.

Balance: cedar

Energy and love: caraway and lime

Energy: garlic, lemon, nasturtium, and saffron

Fertility: musk, mustard, parsley, and sunflower

Fertility and energy: pine

Fertility and love: daffodil, mandrake, mistletoe, poppy, rose, and geranium

Fertility, love, and happiness: geranium

Fertility, sex, and energy: patchouli

Fidelity: spikenard

Fidelity, love, and energy: nutmeg

Friendship: snapdragon

Friendship, strength, love, and happiness: sweet pea

Happiness and peace: lily of the valley

Happiness, harmony, and peace: basil

Happiness, peace, and love: lavender

Honesty and prosperity: honeysuckle

Joy, happiness, and sex: neroli

Love (long-lasting): orris

Love and energy: cinnamon, peppermint, and rosemary

Love and fertility: apple

Love and fidelity: clover

Love and happiness: hyacinth, John the Conqueror, and tulip

Love and marriage: orange blossom

Love and peace: catnip, gardenia, plumeria, spider, lily, stephanotis, valerian, and violet

Love and sex: cardamom

Love and strength: zinnia
Love and truth: cyclamen
Love and vitality: ginseng
Love, energy, and sex: ginger
Love, friendship, and peace: apple blossom
Love, joy, and energy: orange
Love, peace, and sex: jasmine, rose, and ylang-ylang
Love, sex, and energy: vanilla
Love: balm of Gilead, cherry, clove, coriander, damiana, dill, dragon's blood, freesia, hibiscus, iris, juniper, lemon verbena, lilac, lotus, mimosa, mullein, palmarosa, periwinkle, spearmint, primrose, raspberry, rue, strawberry, tonka bean, vetivert, willow, wood, aloe, wormwood, and yarrow
Peace and friendship: passionflower
Peace and harmony: bayberry
Peace and love: meadowsweet
Peace and strength: rhododendron
Peace and tranquility: coltsfoot
Peace, fidelity, and love: magnolia
Peace, happiness, and love: tuberose water lily
Peace, harmony, and love: narcissus
Peace, strength, and energy: pennyroyal
Peace: chamomile, lemon balm, lily, marjoram, and vervain
Prosperity: almond, elderberry, hyssop, and sage
Rituals of celebration: maple
Sex: sandalwood
Stability and peace: amber
Strength: mugwort
Strength and vitality: tangerine
Strength, vitality, energy, and love: carnation

Altar Decorations

What symbols come to mind when you think of your theme? If love is a part of your theme, use hearts or cupids; use doves for peace; use a heavy chain for strength; or try a telephone for communication! An egg or rabbit can be used to signify fertility. A rock can stand for stability or strength. A cornucopia overflowing with fruits and vegetables may represent abundance or prosperity. If you can find one, a weighted scale works perfectly for balance. Use a live plant for growth. Use a feather for sensuality or tenderness.

Because this is a ritual to celebrate an engagement, if there is an engagement ring, now is the time for the ring to be blessed, and it should be placed on your altar. Incorporate the colors you have chosen with flowers, ribbons, and candles. Place a picture of the engaged couple on the altar.

Make a fresh bouquet of your chosen herbs and flowers. Use dried herbs and flowers to crush into incense to burn on a charcoal tab. Pure oils can be dripped onto a lit charcoal tab to release a burst of scent in a beautiful cloud.

Ceremony

Begin your ritual as you normally would with your own version of creating a circle and calling the quarters. Once you have completed your normal ritual opening you may proceed using this sample ritual. You will also use your own closing once you have completed the specific ritual.

Say the following:

Lady of the Moon, Lord of the Woods, please join with us in this rite of celebration as (name) and (name) come forth to announce their intents of love and commitment to one another.

(Name) and (name) have found in each other, a person to love and share their lives with. They wish to be bound together in love and life. As these two come before the Lord and Lady, and all of us to announce their intent of marriage, we wish them a life of love, friendship, and joy. May they always be open and honest with one another, and able to communicate to their hearts' content.

In these days, marriages often fail, and so (God) and (Goddess), we ask for your blessing on this union, that it will have stability, joy, love, and the endurance to see things through. We celebrate in their joy and love for one another.

8

New Car

Some people may find this to be an odd reason for a ritual, but think about it: How much time do you spend in your car driving around? Wouldn't it be nice to know you have someone looking over you to help keep you safe?

These days, cars can be extremely expensive, and we all should show more gratitude for the fact that we are able to afford a car at all! For many people on a tight budget, losing their car could mean losing their job. At the same time, for many people, losing their job could mean losing their car. Continued success and prosperity is a necessity when it comes to being a car owner!

Themes

Choose two or three themes on which to center your ritual.

- ✑ Happiness
- ✑ Protection
- ✑ Prosperity
- ✑ Success

Colors

Choose colors that support your theme. You may also want to include something that is the same color as your new car.

Black: protection   **Orange:** success
Blue: protection   **Pink:** success
Gold: success   **White:** protection
Green: prosperity   **Yellow:** happiness

Crystals and Stones

Choose crystals and stones that support your theme.

Happiness: amethyst and rose quartz
Happiness and success: amazonite
Protection: agate, beryl, citrine, diamond, garnet, jasper, lepidolite, malachite, moonstone, obsidian, onyx, sunstone, turquoise, or zircon
Protection and prosperity: jade, peridot, sapphire, tiger's-eye, topaz, tourmaline, and turquoise
Protection, prosperity, and happiness: chrysoprase and lapis lazuli
Prosperity: emerald and opal
Prosperity and happiness: ruby
Success: malachite

Incense, Oils, and Herbs

Choose incense, oils, and herbs that support your theme.

Happiness: Adam and Eve root, basil, bergamot, buttercup, catnip, celandine, cyclamen, hawthorn, High John thehyacinth, lavender, lily of the valley, marjoram, meadowsweet, saffron, St. John's wort, and witch grass.

Protection: African violet, agrimony, aloe, alyssum, amaranth, anemone, angelica, ash, balm of Gilead, bamboo, barley, basil, bay, birch, bittersweet, blackberry, bladderwrack, bloodroot, blueberry, boneset, broom, buckthorn, buckwheat, burdock, cactus, calamus, caraway, carnation, carob, cascara sagrada, castor, cedar, celandine, chrysanthemum, cinnamon, cinquefoil, clove, clover, club moss, cohosh, cotton, cumin, curry, cypress, devil's bit, devil's shoestring, dill, dogwood, dragon's blood, elder, elecampane, eucalyptus, fennel, fern, feverfew, flax, foxglove, frankincense, galangal, garlic, geranium, ginseng, hazel, heather, holly, honeysuckle, horehound, hyacinth, hyssop, Irish moss, ivy, juniper, kava-kava, lady's slipper, larch, larkspur, lavender, lilac, lily, lily of the valley, liverwart, loosestrife, lotus, mallow, mandrake, marigold, marjoram, mimosa, mint, mistletoe, mugwort, mulberry, mullein, mustard, myrrh, nettle, oak, orris, parsley, pennyroyal, peony, pepper, periwinkle, pine, primrose, ragwort, raspberry, rice, rose, rosemary, rowan, sage, St. John's wort, sandalwood, snapdragon, Solomon's seal, Spanish moss, tamarisk, valerian, vervain, violet, willow, wintergreen, witchhazel, wolfsbane, woodruff, wormwood, yerba santa, and yucca.

Prosperity: alfalfa, almond, ash, benzoin, bergamot, camellia, elder, honeysuckle, and hyssop.

Success: cinnamon, clover, ginger, High John the Conqueror, lemon balm, rowan, and woodruff.

Altar Decorations

This is a small ritual, and the decorations should reflect the size. More than likely, this will be a ritual you will perform on your own, although you can invite family and close friends to help you in your celebration.

If you can, find a toy version of your car, place it on your altar, or you can use a picture.

Your car keys are a direct connection to your car, so these too can be placed on the altar.

Anything you want to use to decorate your car with can also be placed on the altar or in your ritual area, including steering wheel or seat covers, air fresheners, or even custom floor mats.

Incorporate the colors you have chosen with flowers, ribbons, and candles.

Make a fresh bouquet of your chosen herbs and flowers. Crush dried herbs and flowers into incense and burn on a charcoal tab. Pure oils can be dripped onto a lit charcoal tab to release a burst of scent in a beautiful cloud.

Ceremony

Begin your ritual as you normally would with your own version of creating a circle and calling the quarters. Once you have completed your normal ritual opening you may proceed using this sample ritual. You will also use your own closing once you have completed the specific ritual.

Say the following:

> *Lord and Lady, I come to you tonight with both a thank you and a request. I thank you for aiding in my quest for a new car, and ask for your aid in continued success.*
>
> *I also ask for your blessing of protection to keep my car safe, and myself safe when I am using it.*

Pick up the black bag and pass through incense smoke.

> *I ask for your blessings of protection and success, and store them in this bag.*

Place stones in the bag and tie it shut.

> *Lord and Lady, I carry your blessings and love with me.*

Close your ritual and circle in your normal way and place the bag in a safe location in your car, such as in your glove box or in a cup holder. If the bag is small enough, you can tie it your rear-view mirror.

New Job/Promotion

Themes

Choose two or three themes on which to center your ritual.

- Creativity
- Happiness
- Mental powers
- Protection
- Prosperity
- Strength
- Success

Colors

Choose colors that support your theme.

Black: protection
Blue: protection, change, wisdom, and knowledge
Brown: strength
Gold: success and employment
Green: prosperity, employment, and career
Indigo: change
Magenta: change
Orange: success and opportunities

Pink: success
Purple: success
Red: strength
Violet: success
White: protection
Yellow: happiness and creativity

Crystals and Stones

Choose crystals and stones that support your theme.

Creativity: citrine and kunzite
Happiness: amazonite, amethyst, rose quartz, and ruby
Happiness, protection, and prosperity: chrysoprase lapis lazuli
Mental powers: aventurine, chrysocolla, emerald, moldavite, rhodochrosite, rhodonite, and sodalite
Mental powers and protection: diamond and zircon
Mental powers, protection, and prosperity: jade
Prosperity: emerald, opal, ruby
Protection: agate, beryl, citrine, garnet, jasper, lepidolite, moonstone, obsidian, onyx, sunstone, and zircon
Protection and prosperity: peridot, sapphire, tiger's-eye, topaz, tourmaline, and turquoise
Protection and success: malachite
Strength: agate, bloodstone, diamond, garnet, and onyx
Success: amazonite

Incense, Oils, and Herbs

Choose incense, oils, and herbs that support your theme.

Creativity: lemon

Creativity, happiness, and prosperity: bergamot

Happiness: Adam and Eve root, buttercup, catnip, cyclamen, hawthorn, meadowsweet, saffron, and witch grass

Happiness and protection: basil, celandine, hyacinth, lavender, lily of the valley, and marjoram

Happiness and success: High John the Conqueror

Happiness, protection, and strength: St. John's wort

Mental powers: celery seed, iris, rue, spearmint, summer savory, sunflower, vanilla, and walnut

Mental powers and protection: mustard seed, periwinkle, rosemary, and sage

Mental powers and prosperity: almond

Prosperity: alfalfa, benzion, and camellia

Protection: African violet, agrimony, aloe, alyssum, amaranth, anemone, angelica, balm of Gilead, bamboo, barley, birch, bittersweet, blackberry, bladderwrack, bloodroot, blueberry, boneset, broom, buckthorn, buckwheat, burdock, cactus, calamus, caraway, carnation, carob, cascara sagrada, castor, cedar, chrysanthemum, cinquefoil, clove, club moss, cohosh, cotton, cumin, curry, cypress, devil's bit, devil's shoestring, dill, dogwood, dragon's blood, elecampane, eucalyptus, fennel, fern, feverfew, flax, foxglove, frankincense, galangal, garlic, geranium, ginseng, hazel, heather, holly, horehound, Irish moss, ivy, juniper, kava-kava, lady's slipper, larch, larkspur, lilac, lily, liverwart, loosestrife, lotus, mallow, mandrake, marigold, mimosa, mint, mistletoe, mullein, myrrh, nettle, oak, orris, parsley, peony, pepper, pine, primrose, ragwort, raspberry, rice, rose, sandalwood, snapdragon, Solomon's seal, Spanish moss, tamarisk, valerian, vervain, violet, willow, wintergreen, witch hazel, wolfsbane, wormwood, yerba santa, and yucca

Protection and prosperity: ash, elder, honeysuckle, and hyssop

Protection and strength: bay, mugwort, mulberry, and pennyroyal

Strength: saffron and sweetpea

Success: ginger and lemon balm

Success and protection: cinnamon, clover, rowan, and woodruff

Altar Decorations

Getting a new job or receiving a promotion is a great reason to celebrate with a ritual. While you will want to thank the deities for their aid in your success, you will also want to ask them for continued success to do a job well.

Incorporate aspects from your daily work life into your altar decorations. Are there certain tools you use in your work? Place some of these on your altar. Place your company's logo, letterhead, or other work-related items on your altar.

You may also wish to adopt your work dress code for your ritual. If you wear some type of uniform to work, wear it while performing your ritual.

Incorporate the colors you have chosen with flowers, ribbons, and candles.

Make a fresh bouquet of your chosen herbs and flowers. Crush dried herbs and flowers into incense and burn on a charcoal tab. Pure oils can be dripped onto a lit charcoal tab to release a burst of scent in a beautiful cloud.

Ceremony

Begin your ritual as you normally would with your own version of creating a circle and calling the quarters. Once you have completed your normal ritual opening you may proceed using this sample ritual. You will also use your own closing once you have completed the specific ritual.

Say the following:

Lady of light, Lord of the wild, I come to you in celebration of my new promotion. Through your love and guidance, I have, and will, continue to succeed. Bless me and grant me the creativity my position requires as I travel on my road to personal success.

As I take on this new position, with new responsibilities, grant me the strength I will need as I travel on my road to personal success. As I find joy in my chosen career, I will thank you and show gratitude. As I travel on my road to personal success. thank you for opportunities given and blessings received.

10

New Home

Themes

Choose two or three themes on which to center your ritual.

- Comfort
- Happiness
- Hope
- Love
- New beginnings

- Peace
- Prosperity
- Protection
- Security
- Stability

Colors

Choose colors that support your theme.

Black: protection
Blue: protection, hope, and peace
Brown: stability
Green: prosperity and security
Light blue: comfort
Pink: household peace
Silver: stability

White: peace and protection
Yellow: happiness

Crystals and Stones

Choose crystals and stones that support your theme.

Happiness: amazonite
Happiness and prosperity: ruby
Happiness, love, and protection: lapis lazuli
Love and happiness: alexandrite
Love and protection: beryl
Love, peace, and happiness: rose quartz and amethyst
Love, peace, prosperity, and protection: sapphire and tourmaline
Peace: aquamarine, aventurine, calcite, carnelian, and rhodonite
Peace and love: chrysocolla and rhodochrosite
Peace and protection: lepidolite
Prosperity: opal
Prosperity and protection: tiger's-eye
Prosperity, happiness, and protection: chrysoprase
Prosperity, love, and peace: emerald
Protection and peace: zircon
Protection and prosperity: peridot
Protection, love, and peace: malachite and moonstone
Protection, prosperity, and happiness: turquoise
Protection, prosperity, and love: topaz
Protection, prosperity, love, and peace: jade
Protection: agate, citrine, diamond, garnet, jasper, obsidian, onyx, and sunstone

Incense, Oils, and Herbs

Choose incense, oils, and herbs that support your theme.

Comfort and protection: cypress

Happiness: hawthorn and lily of the valley

Love: apple, apricot, bachelor's button, bleeding heart, catnip, cherry, chickweed, coltsfoot, columbine, copal, coriander, crocus, cubeb, daffodil, damiana, ginger, lady's mantle, lemon, lemon verbena, licorice, lovage, maple, orchid, pansy, peppermint, poppy, senna, spearmint, spikenard, strawberry, vetivert, yarrow, and yerba mate

Love and happiness: Adam and Eve root, High John the Conqueror, saffron, and witch grass

Love and peace: gardenia and scullcap

Love and protection: balm of Gilead, barley, basil, bloodroot, clove, clover, dragon's blood, elecampane, geranium, ginseng, lettuce, lime, linden, mallow, mandrake, mimosa, mint, mistletoe, mullein, orris, parsley, periwinkle, primrose, raspberry, rose, rosemary, valerian, willow, and wormwood

Love, peace, and happiness: meadowsweet

Love, protection, and happiness: hyacinth

Love, protection, and peace: vervain and violet

Love, protection, happiness, and peace: lavender

Peace and protection: loosestrife olive

Prosperity: alfalfa almond

Prosperity and love: nuts

Protection: African violet, agrimony, aloe, alyssum, amaranth, anemone, angelica, bamboo, bay, birch, bittersweet, blackberry, blueberry, boneset, broom, buckthorn, buckwheat, burdock, cactus, calamus, caraway, carnation, cascara sagrada, castor, cedar, chrysanthemum, cinnamon, club moss, cotton, cumin, curry, devil's shoestring, dill, eucalyptus, fennel, fern, feverfew, foxglove, frankincense, galangal, garlic, hazel, heather, holly, honeysuckle, horehound, hyssop, Irish moss, juniper, lady's slipper, larkspur, lilac, lily, lotus, marigold, mugwort, mulberry, mustard seed, myrrh, nettle, oak, pennyroyal, peony, pepper, pine, ragwort, rice, rowan, sage, sandalwood, snapdragon, Solomon's seal, Spanish moss, thistle, witch hazel, and yucca

Protection and happiness: celandine and cyclamen
Protection and prosperity: elder
Protection, love, and happiness: marjoram and St. John's wort

Altar Decorations

Your new home requires not only a great celebration, but also a spiritual cleansing to rid it of any negativity that may have been left by the previous occupants.

Because you will be performing a cleansing and blessing of the home, you should perform this ritual inside of the house. Feel free, of course, to have the entire family participate as well as any friends you would like to include.

Because of the nature of this ritual, you may not have many "extra" decorations to include. However, a picture or the people who will be living in the house is a nice extra touch.

Include symbols that represent your themes.

Incorporate the colors you have chosen with flowers, ribbons, and candles.

Make a fresh bouquet of your chosen herbs and flowers. Crush dried herbs and flowers into incense and burn on a charcoal tab. Pure oils can be dripped onto a lit charcoal tab to release a burst of scent in a beautiful cloud.

Ceremony

Begin your ritual as you normally would with your own version of creating a circle and calling the quarters. Once you have completed your normal ritual opening you may proceed using this sample ritual. You will also use your own closing once you have completed the specific ritual.

Say the following:

Lady of the moon, Lady of the light, Lady of the stars, Lady of the night, Lord of the wild, Lord of the green, Lord of the living, Lord of the free, we call upon you to join us as we gather to celebrate and bless our new home.

*We ask for your blessings upon our home, we ask for your
blessings of comfort. We ask for your blessings of peace. We
ask for your blessings of protection. We ask for your blessings of security.*

At this point, pick up the sage and walk throughout each
room of the house, opening all the doors and windows as you go.
This is to give negative entities a way out. As you walk throughout your home, chant the following:

*We consecrate and clear this space. Let nothing but peace,
joy, comfort, and security linger here.*

After walking through the entire house, return to your altar
and say the following:

*We ask for your blessings of comfort. We ask for your
blessings of peace.*

*We ask for your blessings of protection. We ask for
your blessings of security.*

11

Handfasting/ Marriage

Themes

Choose two or three themes on which to center your ritual.

- ✌ Abundance
- ✌ Affection
- ✌ Balance
- ✌ Celebrating life cycles
- ✌ Communication
- ✌ Endurance
- ✌ Energy
- ✌ Fertility
- ✌ Fidelity
- ✌ Friendship
- ✌ Growth

- ✌ Happiness
- ✌ Harmony
- ✌ Honesty
- ✌ Honor
- ✌ Love
- ✌ New beginnings
- ✌ Passion
- ✌ Patience
- ✌ Peace
- ✌ Prosperity
- ✌ Romance

- Security
- Sensuality
- Sex
- Stability
- Strength
- Tranquility
- Truth
- Understanding
- Unity
- Vitality

Colors

Choose colors that support your theme.

Blue: truth, tranquility, honor, peace, fidelity, and unity
Brown: stability, sensuality, endurance, strength, and grace
Gold: vitality and strength
Green: abundance, growth, prosperity, fertility, and security
Light blue: tranquility, patience, and understanding
Orange: enthusiasm, energy, friendship, and communication
Pink: compassion, tenderness, harmony, affection, love, romance, and honor
Purple: growth
Red: sexual love, passion, energy, and strength
Silver: truth, stability, and balance
Turquoise: honor
White: peace, truth, and tranquility
Yellow: joy, vitality, and communication

Crystals and Stones

Choose crystals and stones that support your theme.

Balance: moldavite
Balance and strength: onyx

Communication, peace, and balance: kunzite
Compassion and growth: celestite
Energy: jasper
Energy and love: beryl
Energy, love, and peace: malachite
Energy, peace, love, and balance: rhodochrosite
Fertility: geode
Intensifies energy: clear quartz
Joy: amazonite
Joy, love, fidelity, and prosperity: lapis lazuli
Love and joy: alexandrite
Love, friendship, prosperity, peace, and energy: tourmaline
Love, harmony, and peace: moonstone
Love, peace, and happiness: rose quartz
Love, peace, and prosperity: sapphire
Love, peace, sexual energy, and balance: zircon
Passion and sexuality: sunstone
Peace: aquamarine, aventurine, calcite, and rhodonite
Peace and balance: lepidolite
Peace, happiness, and love: amethyst
Peace, love, communication, and vitality: chrysocolla
Prosperity and balance: opal peridot
Prosperity and joy: ruby
Prosperity, balance, love, and tranquility: topaz
Prosperity, energy, and honesty: tiger's-eye
**Prosperity, friendship, communication, happiness, and
    balance:** turquoise
Prosperity, happiness, and friendship: chrysoprase
Prosperity, love, fertility, and peace: jade
Prosperity, love, peace, and balance: emerald
Sexual energy: citrine

Sexual energy and peace: carnelian
Strength: bloodstone
Strength and love: agate
Strength and sexual abilities: diamond
Strength, energy, and compassion: garnet

Incense, Oils, and Herbs

Choose incense, oils, and herbs that support your theme.

Balance: cedar
Energy: garlic, lemon, nasturtium, and saffron
Energy and love: caraway and lime
Fertility: musk, mustard, parsley, and sunflower
Fertility and energy: pine
Fertility and love: daffodil, mandrake, poppy, and rose geranium
Fertility, love, and happiness: geranium
Fertility, sex, and energy: patchouli
Fidelity, love, and energy: nutmeg
Fidelity: spikenard
Friendship: snapdragon
Friendship, strength, love, and happiness: sweet pea
Happiness and peace: lily of the valley
Happiness, harmony, and peace: basil
Happiness, peace, and love: lavender
Honesty and prosperity: honeysuckle
Joy, happiness, and sex: neroli
Long-lasting love: orris
Love and energy: cinnamon, peppermint, and rosemary
Love and fertility: apple and mistletoe
Love and fidelity: clover

Love and happiness: hyacinth, High John the Conqueror, and tulip

Love and marriage: orange blossom

Love and peace: catnip, gardenia, plumeria, spider, lily, stephanotis, valerian, and violet

Love and sex: cardamom

Love and strength: zinnia

Love and truth: cyclamen

Love and vitality: ginseng

Love, energy, and sex: ginger

Love, friendship, and peace: apple blossom

Love, joy, and energy: orange

Love, peace, and sex: jasmine, rose, and ylang-ylang

Love, sex, and energy: vanilla

Love: balm of Gilead, cherry, clove, coriander, damiana, dill, dragon's blood, freesia, hibiscus, iris, juniper, lemon verbena, lilac, lotus, mimosa, mullein, palmarosa, periwinkle, primrose, raspberry, rue, spearmint, strawberry, tonka bean, vetivert, willow, wood aloe, wormwood, and yarrow

Peace: chamomile, lemon balm, lily, marjoram, and vervain

Peace and friendship: passionflower

Peace and harmony: bayberry

Peace and love: meadowsweet

Peace and strength: rhododendron

Peace and tranquility: coltsfoot

Peace, fidelity, and love: magnolia

Peace, happiness, and love: tuberose and water lily

Peace, harmony, and love: narcissus

Peace, strength, and energy: pennyroyal

Prosperity: almond, elderberry, hyssop, and sage

Rituals of celebration: maple

Sex: sandalwood

Stability and peace: amber
Strength: mugwort
Strength and vitality: tangerine
Strength, vitality, energy, and love: carnation

Altar Decorations

Your handfasting may or may not be a legally binding marriage depending on who is performing the ceremony and the laws in your area. Whether you are using this ritual as a legally binding ceremony or not, it's important to remember that it is *your* day, and should be done the way you and your partner want it to be done. Too often in the world of weddings, family and friends want to chime in and plan everything for you. Be gracious, yet firm, and let everyone know you plan on doing it your way.

Just about anything goes for a handfasting, and the only requirement for an element to be included is that the happy couple wants it. You can choose any colors you want, but your handfasting ribbons should correspond with your themes.

Incorporate the colors you have chosen with flowers, ribbons, and candles.

Handfastings are a wonderful time to incorporate lots of flowers, either real or fake, into your ritual decorations. Make fresh bouquets of your chosen herbs and flowers. If you have an area where they can be used, flower garlands can be draped around the circle or the "audience." Crush dried herbs and flowers into incense and burn on a charcoal tab. Pure oils can be dripped onto a lit charcoal tab to release a burst of scent in a beautiful cloud.

Ceremony

Begin your ritual as you normally would with your own version of creating a circle and calling the quarters. Once you have completed your normal ritual opening you may proceed using this sample ritual. You will also use your own closing once you have completed the specific ritual. This ritual will, of course, require at least a third party to actually perform the ceremony part. You can either perform this ritual for another couple or have someone perform it for you. This is an example of a simple ritual—handfasting rituals can be quaintly simple or extremely extravagant, whichever suits your needs best.

> *Loving Lady, gracious Lord, grant your blessings upon these two, who have come before you, their family, and their friends to join themselves together as one. Through this rite, (name) and (name) will share their promises to one another with one another and all who will listen. We are here with them today, to celebrate, to rejoice, and to support them in their unity. (Name) and (name) have chosen one another to be their long life mate, their partner, their lover, their friend. (Name) and (name), please take one another's hand.*

At this time, the person performing the ceremony will ask the following questions. After both parties have answered, take each corresponding ribbon and lay it over their wrists. After all ribbons have been lain across the wrists the ends should be gathered up in two hands and brought back up around to the top where they will be tied together.

Do you each give your oath to be open and honest, and to do your best to communicate with each other at all times?

Lay yellow ribbon across their wrists.

Do you each give your oath to do your best to surround one another in a tranquil peace?

Lay white ribbon across their wrists.

Do you each give your oath to be understanding through times of difficulties as well as through times of ease?

Lay light blue ribbon across their wrists.

Do you each give your oath to provide for one another and to rejoice in the abundance and fertility provided to you by our Lord and Lady?

Lay green ribbon across their wrists.

Do you each give your oath to love one another with passion in your heart and fire in your soul?

Lay red ribbon across their wrists.

Do you each give your oath to love one another with the romance and tenderness as all lovers should?

Lay pink ribbon across their wrists.

Do you each give your oath of friendship to one another, to provide companionship throughout the days of your lives?

Lay orange ribbon across their wrists.

Tie ribbons together.

Loving Lady and Gracious Lord, as the two of you have come together, (name) and (name) also come together to share their love. We ask for your blessings upon this union as the two have now become one. It is now my pleasure to present unto you Mr. and Mrs. (name), husband and wife.

Close the circle now as you normally would.

12

Menopoause/
Croning

Themes

Choose two or three themes on which to center your ritual.

- Celebrating life cycles
- The Elements
- Happiness
- Honor
- The God
- The Goddess

- Love
- Protection
- Purification
- Spirituality
- Wisdom

Colors

Choose colors that support your theme.

Black: protection

Blue: protection, honor, change, virgin goddesses, wisdom, and
      knowledge
Brown: earth
Gold: the gods and solar deities
Indigo: insight and change
Magenta: intuition and change
Pink: love and honor
Purple: insight, inspiration, and spirituality
Red: life cycle
Silver: the goddesses, intuition, and lunar deities
Turquoise: honor
Violet: intuition and spiritual awareness
White: protection and purification

Colors for the Elements

Earth: black, brown, green, and gold
Air: white, lavender, and pale blue
Water: blue, blue-green, aquamarine, indigo, and white
Fire: red, orange, yellow, and gold

Crystals and Stones

Choose crystals and stones that support your theme.

Happiness and love: amethyst
Happiness and protection: chrysoprase
Intuition: hematite
Joy: amazonite
Love: emerald and rhodochrosite
Love and happiness: rose quartz

Love and protection: agate, beryl, lapis lazuli, moonstone, sapphire, topaz, tourmaline, and zircon

Love, spiritual transformation, and joy: alexandrite

Protection: citrine, jasper, obsidian, onyx, sunstone, tiger's-eye, and turquoise

Protection and intuition: peridot

Protection and love: jade and malachite

Protection and purification: garnet

Protection and spirituality: diamond

Purification: aquamarine and calcite

Spirituality and protection: lepidolite

Wisdom: chrysocolla and sodalite

Incense, Oils, and Herbs

Choose incense, oils, and herbs that support your theme.

Love: apple, aster, bachelor's button, bleeding heart, chickweed, coltsfoot, columbine, and ginger

Love and happiness: Adam and Eve root and catnip

Love and protection: balm of Gilead, barley, basil, lemon verbena, mandrake, and thyme

Love and purification: copal

Love and spirituality: gardenia

Love, protection, and happiness: hyacinth

Love, protection, and purification: bloodroot, parsley, and vervain

Love, protection, purification, and happiness: lavender

Protection and happiness: celandine cyclamen

Protection and love: clover, dragon's blood, elecampane, ginseng, violet, and wormwood

Protection and purification: bay, birch, cedar, fennel, and yucca

Protection, love, and happiness: marjoram
Protection: agrimony, aloe, alyssum, amaranth, anemone, angelica,
 bittersweet, bladderwrack, buckthorn, carnation,
 chrysanthemum, dill, eucalyptus, fern, feverfew,
 geranium, heather, holly, juniper, and lady's slipper
Purification: chamomile
Purification and protection: broom, hyssop, and valerian
Spirituality: cinnamon
Spirituality and protection: African violet
Wisdom, protection, and purification: sage

Altar Decorations

Over the past generations, society (especially in America) has tended to write off elderly people and the wisdom they carry with them. In most Pagan practices, the older generation is revered. They pass their knowledge down to younger people and are respected. This ritual is designed to celebrate the time in a woman's life when she transitions from the aspect of mother to the aspect of crone.

Depending on your own preferences, croning ceremonies can be short and simple or long and more elaborate. You may choose to invite women only, or allow men to participate. In most traditions, if men are allowed to attend, they are there to observe only and do not participate in the actual ritual. This ritual can be changed to be done on your own, but it is highly recommended that you perform this ritual as a group with someone other than the new crone leading the ceremony.

A croning ritual is a very spiritual transformation for the woman involved. She is making a major transition in her life—physically, spiritually, and most likely emotionally.

This ritual should be a sincere event, and the decorations should reflect this.

Place statuary or pictures of Crone aspect goddesses on your altar.

If it is possible (depending on where and how your ritual area is set up), decorate the area surrounding your circle with veils of thin see-through material or scarves. This symbolizes the transition from one aspect to another.

The Croning ritual is a very Goddess- and wisdom-centered ritual, and your decorations should reflect this through symbolism.

Incorporate the colors you have chosen with flowers, ribbons, and candles.

Make a fresh bouquet of your chosen herbs and flowers. Crush dried herbs and flowers into incense and burn on a charcoal tab. Pure oils can be dripped onto a lit charcoal tab to release a burst of scent in a beautiful cloud.

Ceremony

Begin your ritual as you normally would with your own version of creating a circle and calling the quarters. Once you have completed your normal ritual opening you may proceed using this sample ritual. You will also use your own closing once you have completed the specific ritual.

Say the following:

Great Goddess of the moon and Mother to us all, we come to you tonight to celebrate the Croning of (name).

(Name) has passed through many phases of the circle of life, and through her journey, gained knowledge and wisdom, which, in time, she will be able to pass down to others as she teaches and cares for us in her elder role. This is not a role to be taken lightly, as many people will look to you for assistance in important matters.

(Name), do you wish and promise to take on the role of elder for yourself and for your community? (Name), do you wish and promise to take on the role of mentor and teacher to those who look up to you while traversing their path? (Name), do you wish and promise to take on the role of spiritual leader to those members of our community who come to you for guidance?

It is through these promises and your dedication that the love of and for the Goddess is shown. She shall purify and bless you in her own light. She grants you the wisdom and the strength to share your talents, your knowledge, and your life, with others. We are thankful both for her love, and for your love. We are thankful for her wisdom and for your wisdom. We honor the Goddess and we honor you.

13

Passing Over

Themes

Choose two or three themes on which to center your ritual.

- ∽ Celebrating life cycles
- ∽ The Elements
- ∽ The God
- ∽ The Goddess
- ∽ Honor
- ∽ Love
- ∽ Protection
- ∽ Purification
- ∽ Spirituality

Colors

Choose colors that support your theme.

Black: protection
Blue: protection, honor, and change
Brown: earth
Gold: the gods and solar deities
Indigo: change
Magenta: change
Pink: love and honor

Purple: inspiration and spirituality
Red: life cycle
Silver: the goddesses and lunar deities
Turquoise: honor
Violet: spiritual awareness
White: protection and purification

Colors for the Elements

Earth: black, brown, green, and gold
Air: white, lavender, and pale blue
Water: blue, blue-green, aquamarine, indigo, and white
Fire: red, orange, yellow, and gold

Crystals and Stones

Choose crystals and stones that support your theme.

Love: amethyst, emerald, rhodochrosite, and rose quartz
Love and protection: agate, beryl, jade, lapis lazuli, malachite, moonstone, sapphire, topaz, tourmaline, and zircon
Love and spiritual transformation: alexandrite
Protection: chrysoprase, citrine, jasper, obsidian, onyx, peridot, sunstone, tiger's-eye, and turquoise
Protection and purification: garnet
Protection and spirituality: diamond
Purification: aquamarine and calcite
Spirituality and protection: lepidolite

Incense, Oils, and Herbs

Choose incense, oils, and herbs that support your theme.

Love: Adam and Eve root, apple, aster, bachelor's button, bleeding heart, catnip, chickweed, coltsfoot, columbine, and ginger

Love and protection: balm of Gilead, barley, basil, clover, copal, dragon's blood, elecampane, ginseng, hyacinth, mandrake, and marjoram

Love and purification: thyme

Love and spirituality: gardenia

Love, protection, and purification: bloodroot, lavender, parsley, and vervain

Protection: agrimony, aloe, alyssum, amaranth, anemone, angelica, bittersweet, bladderwrack, buckthorn, carnation, celandine, chamomile, chrysanthemum, cyclamen, dill, eucalyptus, fern, feverfew, geranium, heather, holly, juniper, and lady's slipper

Protection and love: violet and wormwood

Protection and purification: bay, birch, broom, cedar, fennel, hyssop, valerian, and yucca

Protection and spirituality: African violet, frankincense, myrrh, and sandalwood

Purification and love: lemon verbena

Spirituality: cinnamon

Wisdom, protection, and purification: sage

Altar Decorations

In most religions and cultures, funerals are extremely sad events. In Pagan practices, though, it's more common to actually celebrate the life of the person who has departed. Most Pagan beliefs involve some sort of reincarnation, so we know the person hasn't so much as "died" but crossed over to a new world, or at least a new type of existence.

Therefore, a crossing over should be a combination of a celebration of the person's life, a good-bye, a remembrance, and a time to honor the person and all of his or her accomplishments.

The best way to incorporate this into your decorations is through pictures taken over the entire life span of the person the crossing over is for.

Also, the apple is a symbol for immortality, so it would be fitting to include apples in your decorations.

You can also hang veils around the ritual area to represent the crossing over between the two worlds.

Use symbols to represent the other themes you have chosen to work with.

Incorporate the colors you have chosen with flowers, ribbons, and candles.

Make a fresh bouquet of your chosen herbs and flowers. Used dried herbs and flowers to crush into incense to burn on a charcoal tab. Pure oils can be dripped onto a lit charcoal tab to release a burst of scent in a beautiful cloud.

Ceremony

Begin your ritual as you normally would with your own version of creating a circle and calling the quarters. Once you have completed your normal ritual opening you may proceed using this sample ritual. You will also use your own closing once you have completed the specific ritual.

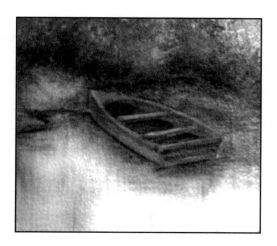

Say the following:

> *Lord of the wild, Lady of the moon, Father and Mother*
> *to us all, we come to you tonight to honor the life of (name),*
> *who lived here on Earth in our presence, and to wish him/*

> her well as we send him/her off on his/her journey through
> the Otherworld. While in our physical presence, (name)
> brought great joy into our lives. While this joy will be missed,
> we take our memories with us as we travel our own paths in
> this life. Our memories of (name) keep him/her alive in our
> minds and our hearts. (Name) now travels on a road we can
> not follow at this time. The distance may bring sadness until
> we merry meet again. At this time we shall share our memo-
> ries of (name).

Each participant should share a meaningful memory of the
departed loved one. After everyone has had a chance to speak,
continue.

> As (name) travels along his/her new path, we send good
> wishes and positive energies and ask for our Lord and Lady
> to watch over him/her and to keep him/her safe. May (name)'s
> journey to the Otherworld be safe and blessed.

PART TWO

Rituals of Nature

14

Sunrise

Themes

Choose two or three themes on which to center your ritual.

- ✎ Celebrating life cycles
- ✎ The Elements
- ✎ The God
- ✎ The Goddess
- ✎ Protection
- ✎ Purification
- ✎ Spirituality
- ✎ The Sun

Colors

Choose colors that support your theme.

Black: protection
Blue: protection and change
Brown: earth
Gold: the gods, the sun, and solar deities
Indigo: change
Magenta: change
Orange: the sun
Purple: inspiration and spirituality

Red: life cycle
Silver: the goddesses
Violet: spiritual awareness
White: protection and purification

Colors for the Elements

Earth: black, brown, green, and gold
Air: white, lavender, and pale blue
Water: blue, blue-green, aquamarine, indigo, and white
Fire: red, orange, yellow, and gold

Crystals and Stones

Choose crystals and stones that support your theme.
Protection and purification: garnet
Protection and spirituality: diamond
Protection: agate, beryl, chrysoprase, citrine, jade, jasper, lapis lazuli,
malachite, moonstone, obsidian, onyx, peridot, sapphire,
sunstone, tiger's-eye, topaz, tourmaline, turquoise, and
zircon
Purification: aquamarine and calcite
Spiritual transformation: alexandrite
Spirituality and protection: lepidolite

Incense, Oils, and Herbs

Choose incense, oils, and herbs that support your theme.
Protection: agrimony, aloe, alyssum, amaranth, anemone, angelica,
balm of Gilead, barley, basil, bittersweet, bladderwrack,

buckthorn, carnation, celandine, chrysanthemum, clover, cyclamen, dill, dragon's blood, elecampane, eucalyptus, fern, feverfew, geranium, ginseng, heather, holly, hyacinth, juniper, lady's slipper, mandrake, marjoram, valerian, violet, and wormwood

Purification and protection: bay, birch, bloodroot, broom, cedar, fennel, hyssop, lavender, parsley, sage, vervain, and yucca

Purification: chamomile, copal, lemon verbena, thyme, and valerian

Spirituality: cinnamon and gardenia

Spirituality and protection: African violet, frankincense, myrrh, and sandalwood

Altar Decorations

Include symbols to represent your themes. You may want to include a statute or picture of your patron God or Goddess. You can also decorate your altar with different statues or pictures of the sun or sunrises.

Incorporate the colors you have chosen with flowers, ribbons and candles.

Make a fresh bouquet of your chosen herbs and flowers. Crush dried herbs and flowers into incense and burn on a charcoal tab. Pure oils can be dripped onto a lit charcoal tab to release a burst of scent in a beautiful cloud.

Ceremony

Begin your ritual as you normally would with your own version of creating a circle and calling the quarters. Once you have completed your normal ritual opening you may proceed using

this sample ritual. You will also use your own closing once you have completed the specific ritual.

Say the following:

> *Oh great God, Father of the day and of me, I come to you this morning to give thanks for this new day, for this moment of new beginnings, for this miracle of a fresh start. I ask for your blessing of protection throughout this day, to keep me safe along with those who I love and who are dear to me. As the sun shines down upon me, it is your warmth that comforts me. As the sun shines down upon me, it is your light that illuminates my way. Protect me and keep me safe in your loving arms, oh mighty Lord of this day.*

15

Sunset

Themes

Choose two or three themes on which to center your ritual.

- Celebrating life cycles
- The Elements
- The God
- The Goddess
- Protection
- Purification
- Spirituality
- The Sun

Colors

Choose colors that support your theme.

Black: protection
Blue: protection and change
Brown: earth
Gold: the gods, the sun, and solar deities
Indigo: change
Magenta: change
Orange: the sun
Purple: inspiration and spirituality
Red: life cycle

Silver: the goddesses
Violet: spiritual awareness
White: protection and purification

Colors for the Elements

Earth: black, brown, green, and gold
Air: white, lavender, and pale blue
Water: blue, blue-green, aquamarine, indigo, and white
Fire: red, orange, yellow, and gold

Crystals and Stones

Choose crystals and stones that support your theme.

Protection: agate, beryl, chrysoprase, citrine, jade, jasper, lapis lazuli, malachite, moonstone, obsidian, onyx, peridot, sapphire, sunstone, tiger's-eye, topaz, tourmaline, turquoise, and zircon
Protection and purification: garnet
Protection and spirituality: diamond and lepidolite
Purification: aquamarine and calcite
Spiritual transformation: alexandrite

Incense, Oils, and Herbs

Choose incense, oils, and herbs that support your theme.

Protection: agrimony, aloe, alyssum, amaranth, anemone, angelica, balm of Gilead, barley, basil, bittersweet, bladderwrack, buckthorn, carnation, celandine, chrysanthemum, clover, cyclamen, dill, dragon's blood, elecampane, eucalyptus, fern,

feverfew, geranium, ginseng, heather, holly, hyacinth, juniper, lady's slipper, mandrake, marjoram, violet, and wormwood

Purification: chamomile, copal, lemon verbena, thyme,

Purification and protection: bay, birch, bloodroot, broom, cedar, fennel, hyssop, lavender, parsley, sage, valerian, vervain, and yucca

Spirituality: cinnamon and gardenia

Spirituality and protection: African violet, frankincense, myrrh, and sandalwood

Altar Decorations

Include symbols to represent your themes. You may want to include a statute or picture of your patron God or Goddess. You can also decorate your altar with different statues or pictures of the sun or sunsets.

Incorporate the colors you have chosen with flowers, ribbons, and candles.

Make a fresh bouquet of your chosen herbs and flowers. Crush dried herbs and flowers into incense and burn on a charcoal tab. Pure oils can be dripped onto a lit charcoal tab to release a burst of scent in a beautiful cloud.

Ceremony

Begin your ritual as you normally would with your own version of creating a circle and calling the quarters. Once you have completed your normal ritual opening you may proceed using

this sample ritual. You will also use your own closing once you have completed the specific ritual.

Say the following:

> *Oh great Goddess, Mother of the day and night and of me, I come to you this evening to give thanks for this past day, for the chance to begin again, for this miracle of a fresh start. As the sun sets upon our world, in this time between time, I ask for your blessing of protection throughout this coming night to keep me safe along with those who I love and who are dear to me. As the sun lays down itself for the night, I follow in its step and lay myself down too. As the sun rests to prepare for another day, I follow in its step and rest myself too. Protect me and keep me safe in your loving arms, oh great Goddess, Mother of mine.*

16

First Snow

Themes

Choose two or three themes on which to center your ritual.

- Celebrating life cycles
- The Elements
- The God
- The Goddess
- Protection
- Purification
- Spirituality

Colors

Choose colors that support your theme.

Black: protection
Blue: protection and change
Brown: earth
Gold: the gods, the sun, and solar deities
Indigo: change
Magenta: change
Orange: the sun
Purple: inspiration and spirituality

Red: life cycle
Silver: the goddesses
Violet: spiritual awareness
White: protection and purification

Colors for the Elements

Earth: black, brown, green, and gold
Air: white, lavender, and pale blue
Water: blue, blue-green, aquamarine, indigo, and white
Fire: red, orange, yellow, and gold

Crystals and Stones

Choose crystals and stones that support your theme.

Protection: agate, beryl, chrysoprase, citrine, jade, jasper, lapis lazuli,
malachite, moonstone, obsidian, onyx, peridot, sapphire,
sunstone, tiger's-eye, topaz, tourmaline, turquoise, and zircon
Spiritual transformation: alexandrite
Purification: aquamarine and calcite
Protection and purification: garnet
Protection and spirituality: diamond and lepidolite

Incense, Oils, and Herbs

Choose incense, oils, and herbs that support your theme.

Protection: agrimony, aloe, alyssum, amaranth, anemone, angelica,
balm of Gilead, barley, basil, bittersweet, bladderwrack,
buckthorn, carnation, celandine, chrysanthemum, clover,
cyclamen, dill, dragon's blood, elecampane, eucalyptus, fern,

feverfew, geranium, ginseng, heather, holly, hyacinth, juniper, lady's slipper, mandrake, marjoram, violet, and wormwood

Purification: chamomile, copal, lemon verbena, and thyme

Purification and protection: bay, birch, bloodroot, broom, cedar, fennel, hyssop, lavender, parsley, sage, valerian, vervain, and yucca

Spirituality: cinnamon and gardenia

Spirituality and protection: African violet, frankincense, myrrh, and sandalwood

Altar Decorations

Decorations for your first snowfall ritual are actually rather self-explanatory—decorate with snowflakes! You can find paper or lace cut-outs, confetti, foam cut-outs, snowflake candles—there are all kinds of snowflake decorations available.

Use symbols to represent the other themes you have chosen.

Incorporate the colors you have chosen with flowers, ribbons, and candles.

Make a fresh bouquet of your chosen herbs and flowers. Used dried herbs and flowers to crush into incense to burn on a charcoal tab. Pure oils can be dripped onto a lit charcoal tab to release a burst of scent in a beautiful cloud.

Ceremony

Begin your ritual as you normally would with your own version of creating a circle and calling the quarters. Once you have completed your normal ritual opening you may proceed using this sample ritual. You will also use your own closing once you have completed the specific ritual.

Say the following:

> *Oh great Goddess, Mother of the moon, tonight I celebrate with you the turning of the wheel. Winter has come, in all her glory as she lets the first snow of the season fall. As the world is blanketed in her chilly embrace, it is warmed at the same time by her promise of a new beginning. When the snow comes, the world around us is washed a new. Impurities and negativities are removed. I come to you tonight to purify myself, my mind, my body, and my thoughts, in a new beginning of my own.*

At this time you will want to perform a quiet meditation to rid your mind of any negative thoughts.

> *As the wheel turns and begins anew, I, too, take the opportunity given to begin my life a new.*

17

Changing of the Leaves

Themes

Choose two or three themes on which to center your ritual.

- ↬ Celebrating life cycles
- ↬ The Elements
- ↬ The God
- ↬ The Goddess
- ↬ Protection
- ↬ Purification
- ↬ Spirituality

Colors

Choose colors that support your theme.

Black: protection
Blue: protection and change
Brown: earth
Gold: the gods, the sun, and solar deities
Indigo: change
Magenta: change
Orange: the sun

Purple: inspiration and spirituality
Red: life cycle
Silver: the goddesses
Violet: spiritual awareness
White: protection and purification

Colors for the Elements

Earth: black, brown, green, and gold
Air: white, lavender, and pale blue
Water: blue, blue-green, aquamarine, indigo, and white
Fire: red, orange, yellow, and gold

Crystals and Stones

Choose crystals and stones that support your theme.

Protection: agate, beryl, chrysoprase, citrine, jade, jasper, lapis lazuli, malachite, moonstone, obsidian, onyx, peridot, sapphire, sunstone, tiger's-eye, topaz, tourmaline, turquoise, and zircon
Protection and purification: garnet
Protection and spirituality: diamond and lepidolite
Purification: aquamarine and calcite
Spiritual transformation: alexandrite

Incense, Oils, and Herbs

Choose incense, oils, and herbs that support your theme.

Protection: agrimony, aloe, alyssum, amaranth, anemone, angelica, balm of Gilead, barley, basil, bittersweet, bladderwrack, buckthorn, carnation, celandine, chrysanthemum, clover, cyclamen, dill, dragon's blood, elecampane, eucalyptus, fern, feverfew, geranium, ginseng, heather, holly, hyacinth, juniper, lady's slipper, mandrake, marjoram, violet, and wormwood

Purification: chamomile, copal, lemon verbena, and thyme

Purification and protection: bay, birch, bloodroot, broom, cedar, fennel, hyssop, lavender, parsley, sage, valerian, vervain, and yucca

Spirituality: cinnamon and gardenia

Spirituality and protection: African violet, frankincense, myrrh, and sandalwood

Altar Decorations

This is another ritual that is easy to decorate for—simply use colored leaves (real if possible, but artificial work just fine). You may also want to add items such as acorns, walnuts, or other nuts or fruits that are ready to be harvested at this time.

Use symbols to represent the other themes you have chosen.

Incorporate the colors you have chosen with flowers, ribbons, and candles.

Make a fresh bouquet of your chosen herbs and flowers. Crush dried herbs and flowers into incense and burn on a charcoal tab. Pure oils can be dripped onto a lit charcoal tab to release a burst of scent in a beautiful cloud.

This sample ritual shows you how simple a ritual can be.

Ceremony

Begin your ritual as you normally would with your own version of creating a circle and calling the quarters. Once you have completed your normal ritual opening you may proceed using this sample ritual. You will also use your own closing once you have completed the specific ritual.

Say the following:

> *Oh great Lady and great Lord, the wheel is forever turning, and now we see it in your eyes. The leaves have found new color, a color brought on by the change of the*

seasons. The world is vibrant and colorful now, a sign of changes to come. The weather will soon become much colder and we take this time to prepare for the winter, as you, Lord and Lady, prepare for a winter of your own. It is through your preparations and sacrifice that we learn how to prepare and what we must sacrifice. Winter is a time of rest and death, with rebirth occurring in spring. As our Lord prepares to leave us, and our Lady prepares to mourn, the world prepares for slumber until our Lord awakes us again with the sun.

18

Spring Blossoms

Themes

Choose two or three themes on which to center your ritual.

- Celebrating life cycles
- Protection
- The Elements
- Purification
- The God
- Spirituality
- The Goddess

Colors

Choose colors that support your theme.

Black: protection
Blue: protection and change
Brown: earth
Gold: the gods, the sun, and solar deities
Indigo: change
Magenta: change
Orange: the sun

Purple: inspiration and spirituality
Red: life cycle
Silver: the goddesses
Violet: spiritual awareness
White: protection and purification

Colors for the Elements

Earth: black, brown, green, and gold
Air: white, lavender, and pale blue
Water: blue, blue-green, aquamarine, indigo, and white
Fire: red, orange, yellow, and gold

Crystals and Stones

Choose crystals and stones that support your theme.

Protection: agate, beryl, chrysoprase, citrine, jade, jasper, lapis lazuli, malachite, moonstone, obsidian, onyx, peridot, sapphire, sunstone, tiger's-eye, topaz, tourmaline, turquoise, and zircon

Protection and purification: garnet
Protection and spirituality: diamond and lepidolite
Purification: aquamarine and calcite
Spiritual transformation: alexandrite

Incense, Oils, and Herbs

Choose incense, oils, and herbs that support your theme.

Protection: agrimony, aloe, alyssum, amaranth, anemone, angelica, balm of Gilead, barley, basil, bittersweet, bladderwrack,

buckthorn, carnation, celandine, chrysanthemum, clover, cyclamen, dill, dragon's blood, elecampane, eucalyptus, fern, feverfew, geranium, ginseng, heather, holly, hyacinth, juniper, lady's slipper, mandrake, marjoram, violet, and wormwood

Purification: chamomile, copal, lemon verbena, and thyme

Purification and protection: bay, birch, bloodroot, broom, cedar, fennel, hyssop, lavender, parsley, sage, valerian, vervain, and yucca

Spirituality: cinnamon and gardenia

Spirituality and protection: African violet, frankincense, myrrh, and sandalwood

Altar Decorations

The best way to decorate for this ritual would be with spring blooming flowers. Although you can use artificial flowers, you really should stop by the store and pick up at least a few real flowers to include on your altar. If you have a flower garden, instead of picking flowers for your altar, hold your ritual either in or right next to the garden. Why settle for a few flowers on the altar when you can have an entire ritual area filled with them?

Use symbols to represent the other themes you have chosen.

Incorporate the colors you have chosen with flowers, ribbons, and candles.

Make a fresh bouquet of your chosen herbs and flowers. Crush dried herbs and flowers into incense and burn on a charcoal tab. Pure oils can be dripped onto a lit charcoal tab to release a burst of scent in a beautiful cloud.

Ceremony

Begin your ritual as you normally would with your own version of creating a circle and calling the quarters. Once you have completed your normal ritual opening you may proceed using this sample ritual. You will also use your own closing once you have completed the specific ritual.

Say the following:

> *Lady of the flowers, Lord of the trees, we welcome you back as the Earth is reborn. Your flowers spring forth from the thawing ground. The God has been reborn and the Goddess no longer mourns. Life is now showing all around us as winter fades away into a warming spring. As the Earth blooms and comes to life again, so do we. We begin to plan for our future and plant seeds that will take root in our minds, our hearts, and our souls. As these seeds grow and change, we watch the world around us change. The wheel turns again.*

19

Summer Warmth

Themes

Choose two or three themes on which to center your ritual.

- Celebrating life cycles
- The Elements
- The God
- The Goddess
- Protection
- Purification
- Spirituality

Colors

Choose colors that support your theme.

Black: protection
Blue: protection and change
Brown: earth
Gold: the gods, the sun, and solar deities
Indigo: change
Magenta: change
Orange: the sun

Purple: inspiration and spirituality
Red: life cycle
Silver: the goddesses
Violet: spiritual awareness
White: protection and purification

Colors for the Elements

Earth: black, brown, green, and gold
Air: white, lavender, and pale blue
Water: blue, blue-green, aquamarine, indigo, and white
Fire: red, orange, yellow, and gold

Crystals and Stones

Choose crystals and stones that support your theme.

Protection: agate, beryl, chrysoprase, citrine, jade, jasper, lapis lazuli, malachite, moonstone, obsidian, onyx, peridot, sapphire, sunstone, tiger's-eye, topaz, tourmaline, turquoise, and zircon
Spiritual transformation: alexandrite
Purification: aquamarine
Purification: calcite
Protection and purification: garnet
Protection and spirituality: diamond
Spirituality and protection: lepidolite

Incense, Oils, and Herbs

Choose incense, oils, and herbs that support your theme.

Protection: agrimony, aloe, alyssum, amaranth, anemone, angelica, balm of Gilead, barley, basil, bittersweet, bladderwrack, buckthorn, carnation, celandine, chrysanthemum, clover, cyclamen, dill, dragon's blood, elecampane, eucalyptus, fern, feverfew, geranium, ginseng, heather, holly, hyacinth, juniper, lady's slipper, mandrake, marjoram, violet, and wormwood

Purification: chamomile, copal, lemon verbena, and thyme

Purification and protection: bay, birch, bloodroot, broom, cedar, fennel, hyssop, lavender, parsley, sage, valerian, vervain, and yucca

Spirituality: cinnamon and gardenia

Spirituality and protection: African violet, frankincense, myrrh, and sandalwood

Altar Decorations

Your ritual celebrating the warmth of the sun should of course include sun symbols, such as statues, pictures, or even sunflowers.

Use symbols to represent your other chosen themes.

Incorporate the colors you have chosen with flowers, ribbons, and candles.

Make a fresh bouquet of your chosen herbs and flowers. Crush dried herbs and flowers into incense and burn on a charcoal tab. Pure oils can be dripped onto a lit charcoal tab to release a burst of scent in a beautiful cloud.

Ceremony

Begin your ritual as you normally would with your own version of creating a circle and calling the quarters. Once you have completed your normal ritual opening you may proceed using this sample ritual. You will also use your own closing once you have completed the specific ritual.

Say the following:

> *Now is the time when the sun is at its strongest. It shines down upon us and we can feel that summer is truly here. As the sun grows to its full strength, so does our Lord. It is through his strength that we are comforted by the warmth of the sun. It is through his strength that each of us finds strength. It is through his strength that we shine a ray of light within each one of us, and take a look at what's inside. This shining light opens our eyes, our minds, our hearts, our souls. This ray of light cleanses our minds, our hearts, our souls. This ray of light purifies our minds, our hearts, our souls. Once again, we are whole.*

20

Celebration of Water

Themes

Choose two or three themes on which to center your ritual.

- ∞ Celebrating life cycles
- ∞ The Elements
- ∞ The God
- ∞ The Goddess
- ∞ Protection
- ∞ Purification
- ∞ Spirituality

Colors

Choose colors that support your theme.

Black: protection
Blue: protection and change
Brown: earth
Gold: the gods, the sun, and solar deities
Indigo: change
Magenta: change

Orange: the sun
Purple: inspiration and spirituality
Red: life cycle
Silver: the goddesses
Violet: spiritual awareness
White: protection and purification

Colors for the Elements

Earth: black, brown, green, and gold
Air: white, lavender, and pale blue
Water: blue, blue-green, aquamarine, indigo, and white
Fire: red, orange, yellow, and gold

Crystals and Stones

Choose crystals and stones that support your theme.

Protection: agate, beryl, chrysoprase, citrine, jade, jasper, lapis lazuli, malachite, moonstone, obsidian, onyx, peridot, sapphire, sunstone, tiger's-eye, topaz, tourmaline, turquoise, and zircon
Protection and purification: garnet
Protection and spirituality: diamond and lepidolite
Purification: aquamarine and calcite
Spiritual transformation: alexandrite

Incense, Oils, and Herbs

Choose incense, oils, and herbs that support your theme.

Protection: agrimony, aloe, alyssum, amaranth, anemone, angelica, balm of Gilead, barley, basil, bittersweet, bladderwrack, buckthorn, carnation, celandine, chrysanthemum, clover, cyclamen, dill, dragon's blood, elecampane, eucalyptus, fern, feverfew, geranium, ginseng, heather, holly, hyacinth, juniper, lady's slipper, mandrake, marjoram, violet, and wormwood

Purification: chamomile, copal, lemon verbena, and thyme

Purification and protection: bay, birch, bloodroot, broom, cedar, fennel, hyssop, lavender, parsley, sage, valerian, vervain, and yucca

Spirituality: cinnamon and gardenia

Spirituality and protection: African violet, frankincense, myrrh, and sandalwood

Altar Decorations

The celebration of water ritual will, of course, need to represent water. Use the colors listed that are associated with water. You may include the other elements if you wish, but the emphasis should be on water.

A tabletop fountain is perfect for this type of ritual, but if you don't have that available, a clear, glass bowl with water in it will suffice.

Use symbols to represent the themes with which you have chosen to work.

Incorporate the colors you have chosen with flowers, ribbons, and candles.

Make a fresh bouquet of your chosen herbs and flowers. Crush dried herbs and flowers into incense and burn on a charcoal tab. Pure oils can be dripped onto a lit charcoal tab to release a burst of scent in a beautiful cloud.

Ceremony

Begin your ritual as you normally would with your own version of creating a circle and calling the quarters. Once you have completed your normal ritual opening you may proceed using this sample ritual. You will also use your own closing once you have completed the specific ritual.

Say the following:

> *Beautiful Lady, Mother to us all, I come to you today in celebration of the element of water. Water is our life-giving force. We are made of water, and can not survive without it. Water cleanses and purifies us. Water rules our emotions, it rules our feelings of love and sorrow. It rules our intuition along with our conscious and unconscious minds. It is a symbol of the womb and fertility. We are as much a part of water as water is a part of us. Through your oceans, lakes, rivers, springs, and wells, you bless us with the abundance of water. It is our responsibility to protect it, a responsibility that should not be taken lightly, but often is.*

Sprinkle some water on your forehead and the top of your head.

> *This water, gift from the Goddess, purifies me in her love and in her light. In return I vow to conserve and protect this natural resource entrusted to our care.*

21

Celebration of Earth

Themes

Choose two or three themes on which to center your ritual.

- ✌ Celebrating life cycles
- ✌ The Elements
- ✌ The God
- ✌ The Goddess
- ✌ Protection
- ✌ Purification
- ✌ Spirituality

Colors

Choose colors that support your theme.

Black: protection
Blue: protection and change
Brown: earth
Gold: the gods, the sun, and solar deities
Indigo: change
Magenta: change
Orange: the sun

Purple: inspiration and spirituality
Red: life cycle
Silver: the goddesses
Violet: spiritual awareness
White: protection and purification

Colors for the Elements

Earth: black, brown, green, and gold
Air: white, lavender, and pale blue
Water: blue, blue-green, aquamarine, indigo, and white
Fire: red, orange, yellow, and gold

Crystals and Stones

Choose crystals and stones that support your theme.

Protection: agate, beryl, chrysoprase, citrine, jade, jasper, lapis lazuli, malachite, moonstone, obsidian, onyx, peridot, sapphire, sunstone, tiger's-eye, topaz, tourmaline, turquoise, and zircon
Protection and purification: garnet
Protection and spirituality: diamond lepidolite
Purification: aquamarine calcite
Spiritual transformation: alexandrite

Incense, Oils, and Herbs

Choose incense, oils, and herbs that support your theme.

Protection: agrimony, aloe, alyssum, amaranth, anemone, angelica, balm of Gilead, barley, basil, bittersweet, bladderwrack,

buckthorn, carnation, celandine, chrysanthemum, clover, cyclamen, dill, dragon's blood, elecampane, eucalyptus, fern, feverfew, geranium, ginseng, heather, holly, hyacinth, juniper, lady's slipper, mandrake, marjoram, violet, and wormwood

Purification: chamomile, copal, lemon verbena, and thyme

Purification and protection: bay, birch, bloodroot, broom, cedar, fennel, hyssop, lavender, parsley, sage, valerian, vervain, and yucca

Spirituality: cinnamon and gardenia

Spirituality and protection: African violet, frankincense, myrrh, and sandalwood

Altar Decorations

The celebration of earth ritual needs decorations that represent earth. Use the colors listed that are associated with earth. You may include the other elements if you wish, but the emphasis should be on earth.

Clear, glass bowls can be filled with soil, salt, or sand. Because stones and crystals come from the earth, you will want to include as many as these as possible.

Use symbols to represent the themes with which you have chosen to work.

Incorporate the colors you have chosen with flowers, ribbons, and candles.

Make a fresh bouquet of your chosen herbs and flowers. Crush dried herbs and flowers into incense and burn on a charcoal tab. Pure oils can be dripped onto a lit charcoal tab to release a burst of scent in a beautiful cloud.

Ceremony

Begin your ritual as you normally would with your own version of creating a circle and calling the quarters. Once you have completed your normal ritual opening you may proceed using this sample ritual. You will also use your own closing once you have completed the specific ritual.

Say the following:

> *Lord and Lady of the earth, you bless us with the stability and grounding energies of the earth. The earth that gives us our crops and fields and grain, the earth that grows our food, the earth that feeds our animals, the earth that feeds and sustains us, the earth that is our home. In many ways, the earth provides for us and keeps us safe. We are protected through her resources and energies. We are entrusted to her care for only a short while and then we leave this earth to our descendents to come. In turn, we are blessed to be her caretakers and must show her the gratitude and respect she rightly deserves. We give our oath to protect and care for our Mother Earth, as she has protected and cared for us.*

22

Celebration of Air

Themes

Choose two or three themes on which to center your ritual.

- ↝ Celebrating life cycles
- ↝ The Elements
- ↝ The God
- ↝ The Goddess
- ↝ Protection
- ↝ Purification
- ↝ Spirituality

Colors

Choose colors that support your theme.

Black: protection
Blue: protection and change
Brown: earth
Gold: the gods, the sun, and solar deities
Indigo: change
Magenta: change
Orange: the sun
Purple: inspiration and spirituality

Red: life cycle
Silver: the goddesses
Violet: spiritual awareness
White: protection and purification

Colors for the Elements

Earth: black, brown, green, and gold
Air: white, lavender, and pale blue
Water: blue, blue-green, aquamarine, indigo, and white
Fire: red, orange, yellow, and gold

Crystals and Stones

Choose crystals and stones that support your theme.

Protection: agate, beryl, chrysoprase, citrine, jade, jasper, lapis lazuli,
malachite, moonstone, obsidian, onyx, peridot, sapphire,
sunstone, tiger's-eye, topaz, tourmaline, turquoise, and
zircon
Protection and purification: garnet
Protection and spirituality: diamond lepidolite
Purification: aquamarine calcite
Spiritual transformation: alexandrite

Incense, Oils, and Herbs

Choose incense, oils, and herbs that support your theme.

Protection: agrimony, aloe, alyssum, amaranth, anemone, angelica,
balm of Gilead, barley, basil, bittersweet, bladderwrack,
buckthorn, carnation, celandine, chrysanthemum, clover,

cyclamen, dill, dragon's blood, elecampane, eucalyptus, fern, feverfew, geranium, ginseng, heather, holly, hyacinth, juniper, lady's slipper, mandrake, marjoram, violet, and wormwood

Purification: chamomile, copal, lemon verbena, and thyme

Purification and protection: bay, birch, bloodroot, broom, cedar, fennel, hyssop, lavender, parsley, sage, valerian, vervain, and yucca

Spirituality: cinnamon and gardenia

Spirituality and protection: African violet, frankincense, myrrh, and sandalwood

Altar Decorations

This ritual needs decorations that remind you of air. Use the colors listed that are associated with this element. Although you may include the other elements if you wish, the emphasis should be on earth.

Air can be represented with clouds, balloons (there is air inside of them!), windsocks set up around the ritual area, steam, mist, smoke, or fog—yes, you can use a fog machine in your ritual!

Use symbols to represent the themes with which you have chosen to work.

Incorporate the colors you have chosen with flowers, ribbons, and candles.

Make a fresh bouquet of your chosen herbs and flowers. Used dried herbs and flowers to crush into incense to burn on a charcoal tab. Pure oils can be dripped onto a lit charcoal tab to release a burst of scent in a beautiful cloud.

Ceremony

Begin your ritual as you normally would with your own version of creating a circle and calling the quarters. Once you have completed your normal ritual opening you may proceed using this sample ritual. You will also use your own closing once you have completed the specific ritual.

Say the following:

> *Lady of the moon, Mother of the earth, you have breathed life into all of us. From our first breath to our last, you nourish us. Your touch is felt when wind blows against*

my skin. Your dance is seen when wind rustles the leaves on the trees. The aromas of your flowers are carried to me on a warm summer's breeze. Your voice whistles through the skies. As the Goddess creates, she also destroys, with ruinous winds, she roars across the land, to wipe her slate clean, and start over again.

23

Celebration of Fire

Themes

Choose two or three themes on which to center your ritual.

- ✦ Celebrating life cycles
- ✦ The Elements
- ✦ The God
- ✦ The Goddess
- ✦ Protection
- ✦ Purification
- ✦ Spirituality

Colors

Choose colors that support your theme.

Black: protection
Blue: protection and change
Brown: earth
Gold: the gods, the sun, and solar deities
Indigo: change
Magenta: change
Orange: the sun

Purple: inspiration and spirituality
Red: life cycle
Silver: the goddesses
Violet: spiritual awareness
White: protection and purification

Colors for the Elements

Earth: black, brown, green, and gold
Air: white, lavender, and pale blue
Water: blue, blue-green, aquamarine, indigo, and white
Fire: red, orange, yellow, and gold

Crystals and Stones

Choose crystals and stones that support your theme.

Protection: agate, beryl, chrysoprase, citrine, jade, jasper, lapis
lazuli, malachite, moonstone, obsidian, onyx, peridot,
sapphire, sunstone, tiger's-eye, topaz, tourmaline,
turquoise, and zircon
Protection and purification: garnet
Protection and spirituality: diamond lepidolite
Purification: aquamarine calcite
Spiritual transformation: alexandrite

Incense, Oils, and Herbs

Choose incense, oils, and herbs that support your theme.

Protection: agrimony, aloe, alyssum, amaranth, anemone, angelica,
balm of Gilead, barley, basil, bittersweet, bladderwrack,

buckthorn, carnation, celandine, chrysanthemum, clover, cyclamen, dill, dragon's blood, elecampane, eucalyptus, fern, feverfew, geranium, ginseng, heather, holly, hyacinth, juniper, lady's slipper, mandrake, marjoram, violet, and wormwood

Purification: chamomile, copal, lemon verbena, and thyme

Purification and protection: bay, birch, bloodroot, broom, cedar, fennel, hyssop, lavender, parsley, sage, valerian, vervain, and yucca

Spirituality: cinnamon and gardenia

Spirituality and protection: African violet, frankincense, myrrh, and sandalwood

Altar Decorations

The celebration of fire ritual needs decorations that represent fire. Use the colors listed that are associated with fire. You may include the other elements if you wish, but the emphasis should be on fire.

It would be ideal for this ritual to be performed near a bonfire. If that is not possible, if you have a large enough cauldron, you can build a small fire inside of it as long as it is safe to do so.

Use plenty of candles on your altar for this ritual.

Pictures of fire, lava, volcanoes, or even the sun, will work well as symbols. Dragons are also a symbol of fire.

Use symbols to represent the themes with which you have chosen to work.

Incorporate the colors you have chosen with flowers, ribbons, and candles.

Make a fresh bouquet of your chosen herbs and flowers. Crush dried herbs and flowers into incense and burn on a charcoal tab. Pure oils can be dripped onto a lit charcoal tab to release a burst of scent in a beautiful cloud.

Ceremony

Begin your ritual as you normally would with your own version of creating a circle and calling the quarters. Once you have completed your normal ritual opening you may proceed using this sample ritual. You will also use your own closing once you have completed the specific ritual.

Say the following:

> *Lord of the Lords and Spirits of the fire, I call upon you to join me in this rite of celebration. In ancient days, fire and life were far more intertwined than what we see today. Over the generations, we have come to take your power for*

granted. *We must remind ourselves of your strength, your comfort, your beauty, your warmth, your protection, your purity, your devastation. You consume all that touch, never deciding good or evil, for you, all is equal.*

24

New Moon

Themes

Choose two or three themes on which to center your ritual.

- ❧ Celebrating life cycles
- ❧ The Elements
- ❧ The God
- ❧ The Goddess
- ❧ Protection
- ❧ Purification
- ❧ Spirituality

Colors

Choose colors that support your theme.

Black: protection
Blue: protection and change
Brown: earth
Gold: the gods, the sun, and solar deities
Indigo: change
Magenta: change
Orange: the sun
Purple: inspiration and spirituality
Red: life cycle

Silver: the goddesses
Violet: spiritual awareness
White: protection and purification

Colors for the Elements

Earth: black, brown, green, and gold
Air: white, lavender, and pale blue
Water: blue, blue-green, aquamarine, indigo, and white
Fire: red, orange, yellow, and gold

Crystals and Stones

Choose crystals and stones that support your theme.

Protection: agate, beryl, chrysoprase, citrine, jade, jasper, lapis lazuli, malachite, moonstone, obsidian, onyx, peridot, sapphire, sunstone, tiger's-eye, topaz, tourmaline, turquoise, and zircon
Protection and purification: garnet
Protection and spirituality: diamond lepidolite
Purification: aquamarine calcite
Spiritual transformation: alexandrite

Incense, Oils, and Herbs

Choose incense, oils, and herbs that support your theme.

Protection: agrimony, aloe, alyssum, amaranth, anemone, angelica, balm of Gilead, barley, basil, bittersweet, bladderwrack, buckthorn, carnation, celandine, chrysanthemum, clover, cyclamen, dill, dragon's blood, elecampane, eucalyptus, fern,

feverfew, geranium, ginseng, heather, holly, hyacinth, juniper, lady's slipper, mandrake, marjoram, violet, and wormwood

Purification: chamomile, copal, lemon verbena, and thyme

Purification and protection: bay, birch, bloodroot, broom, cedar, fennel, hyssop, lavender, parsley, sage, valerian, vervain, and yucca

Spirituality: cinnamon and gardenia

Spirituality and protection: African violet, frankincense, myrrh, and sandalwood

Altar Decorations

Because the moon is not visible when it is new, you probably don't want to use actual moon decorations. You can however cut black circles out to represent the shadowed moon.

Use symbols to represent your chosen themes.

Incorporate the colors you have chosen with flowers, ribbons, and candles.

Make a fresh bouquet of your chosen herbs and flowers. Crush dried herbs and flowers into incense and burn on a charcoal tab. Pure oils can be dripped onto a lit charcoal tab to release a burst of scent in a beautiful cloud.

Ceremony

Begin your ritual as you normally would with your own version of creating a circle and calling the quarters. Once you have completed your normal ritual opening you may proceed using

this sample ritual. You will also use your own closing once you have completed the specific ritual.

Say the following:

Lady of the moon, so dark now in the sky, you are hidden from our view. Yet, we know you are still with us, looking down upon us, protecting us. Soon you will begin to peek out from the darkness and grow until full, to shine your bright light upon us. We come to you now to ask for your blessings, your blessings of wisdom and love. Your blessings to purify our hearts, purify our souls, and purify our minds. Through your darkness you remind us once again of how the wheel turns. All that lives must die, but then will live again as the wheel turns, it is the spiral of life.

25

Full Moon

Themes

Choose two or three themes on which to center your ritual.

- ☙ Celebrating life cycles
- ☙ The Elements
- ☙ The God
- ☙ The Goddess
- ☙ Protection
- ☙ Purification
- ☙ Spirituality

Colors

Choose colors that support your theme.

Black: protection
Blue: protection and change
Brown: earth
Gold: the gods, the sun, and solar deities
Indigo: change
Magenta: change
Orange: the sun
Purple: inspiration and spirituality

Red: life cycle
Silver: the goddesses
Violet: spiritual awareness
White: protection and purification

Colors for the Elements

Earth: black, brown, green, and gold
Air: white, lavender, and pale blue
Water: blue, blue-green, aquamarine, indigo, and white
Fire: red, orange, yellow, and gold

Crystals and Stones

Choose crystals and stones that support your theme.

Protection: agate, beryl, chrysoprase, citrine, jade, jasper, lapis lazuli, malachite, moonstone, obsidian, onyx, peridot, sapphire, sunstone, tiger's-eye, topaz, tourmaline, turquoise, and zircon
Protection and purification: garnet
Protection and spirituality: diamond lepidolite
Purification: aquamarine calcite
Spiritual transformation: alexandrite

Incense, Oils, and Herbs

Choose incense, oils, and herbs that support your theme.

Protection: agrimony, aloe, alyssum, amaranth, anemone, angelica, balm of Gilead, barley, basil, bittersweet, bladderwrack, buckthorn, carnation, celandine, chrysanthemum, clover,

cyclamen, dill, dragon's blood, elecampane, eucalyptus, fern,
feverfew, geranium, ginseng, heather, holly, hyacinth,
juniper, lady's slipper, mandrake, marjoram, violet, and
wormwood

Purification: chamomile, copal, lemon verbena, and thyme

Purification and protection: bay, birch, bloodroot, broom, cedar,
fennel, hyssop, lavender, parsley, sage, valerian, vervain, and
yucca

Spirituality: cinnamon and gardenia

Spirituality and protection: African violet, frankincense, myrrh,
and sandalwood

Altar Decorations

Now that the moon is full, you can include full moon statues
or pictures, full moon confetti, or hang moon shapes above the
ritual space. Use symbols to represent the other themes you have
chosen.

Incorporate the colors you have chosen with flowers, ribbons, and candles.

Make a fresh bouquet of your chosen herbs and flowers.
Crush dried herbs and flowers into incense and burn on a charcoal tab. Pure oils can be dripped onto a lit charcoal tab to release
a burst of scent in a beautiful cloud.

Ceremony

Begin your ritual as you normally would with your own version of creating a circle and calling the quarters. Once you have

completed your normal ritual opening you may proceed using this sample ritual. You will also use your own closing once you have completed the specific ritual.

Say the following:

> *This is the time of the full moon, when its power is at full strength, when its energy is highest. I stand tonight at this altar as a daughter of the moon. I am of the Goddess, I am a daughter of the moon.*
>
> *I come to you to learn, to live in the ways of old. I am of the Goddess, I am a daughter of the moon.*
>
> *I feel your strength and spirit as it flows through me. I am of the Goddess, I am a daughter of the moon.*
>
> *I come to you in love to find the passion inside me. I am of the Goddess, I am a daughter of the moon.*

I come to you for knowledge, for the wisdom of the ages. I am of the Goddess, I am a daughter of the moon.

I come to learn the mysteries of my ancestors long gone. I am of the Goddess, I am a daughter of the moon.

I come to you in peace, to find the peace inside me. I am of the Goddess, I am a daughter of the moon.

I come to you in love, to find the love inside me. I am of the Goddess, I am a daughter of the moon.

I come to you in honor, to find the honor in me. I am of the Goddess, I am a daughter of the moon.

This is the time of the full moon, when its power is at full strength, when its energy is highest. I stand tonight at this altar as a daughter of the moon.

I am of the Goddess, I am a daughter of the moon.

26

Lunar Eclipse

Themes

Choose two or three themes on which to center your ritual.

- Celebrating life cycles
- The Elements
- The God
- The Goddess
- Protection
- Purification
- Spirituality

Colors

Choose colors that support your theme.

Black: protection
Blue: protection and change
Brown: earth
Gold: the gods, the sun, and solar deities
Indigo: change
Magenta: change
Orange: the sun

Purple: inspiration and spirituality
Red: life cycle
Silver: the goddesses
Violet: spiritual awareness
White: protection and purification

Colors for the Elements

Earth: black, brown, green, and gold
Air: white, lavender, and pale blue
Water: blue, blue-green, aquamarine, indigo, and white
Fire: red, orange, yellow, and gold

Crystals and Stones

Choose crystals and stones that support your theme.

Protection: agate, beryl, chrysoprase, citrine, jade, jasper, lapis
    lazuli, malachite, moonstone, obsidian, onyx, peridot,
    sapphire, sunstone, tiger's-eye, topaz, tourmaline,
    turquoise, and zircon
Protection and purification: garnet
Protection and spirituality: diamond lepidolite
Purification: aquamarine calcite
Spiritual transformation: alexandrite

Incense, Oils, and Herbs

Choose incense, oils, and herbs that support your theme.

Protection: agrimony, aloe, alyssum, amaranth, anemone, angelica,
    balm of Gilead, barley, basil, bittersweet, bladderwrack,

buckthorn, carnation, celandine, chrysanthemum, clover, cyclamen, dill, dragon's blood, elecampane, eucalyptus, fern, feverfew, geranium, ginseng, heather, holly, hyacinth, juniper, lady's slipper, mandrake, marjoram, violet, and wormwood

Purification: chamomile, copal, lemon verbena, and thyme

Purification and protection: bay, birch, bloodroot, broom, cedar, fennel, hyssop, lavender, parsley, sage, valerian, vervain, and yucca

Spirituality: cinnamon and gardenia

Spirituality and protection: African violet, frankincense, myrrh, and sandalwood

Altar Decorations

This is not a ritual you will have many opportunities to perform, as lunar eclipses are not everyday occurrences. You can use pictures of any lunar eclipse or make your own by gluing a black circle to a white circle.

Use symbols to represent your other themes.

Incorporate the colors you have chosen with flowers, ribbons, and candles.

Make a fresh bouquet of your chosen herbs and flowers. Crush dried herbs and flowers into incense and burn on a charcoal tab. Pure oils can be dripped onto a lit charcoal tab to release a burst of scent in a beautiful cloud.

Ceremony

Begin your ritual as you normally would with your own version of creating a circle and calling the quarters. Once you have completed your normal ritual opening you may proceed using this sample ritual. You will also use your own closing once you have completed the specific ritual.

Say the following:

> *Lovely Lady, Goddess of all, tonight the moon takes on two faces. It is the full moon, it is the new moon. It is both and it is neither.*
>
> *It is a time between times and a place between places. It is both and it is neither.*
>
> *It is old and it is new. It is both and it is neither.*
>
> *It is light and it is dark. It is both and it is neither.*
>
> *Tonight the moon hides behind the shadow of the earth. We are without her light, we must look to the stars to illuminate the night. For a brief time, we see her in our shadow. But then, she pulls through and her strength shines once again.*

27

Solar Eclipse

Themes

Choose two or three themes on which to center your ritual.

- Celebrating life cycles
- The Elements
- The God
- The Goddess
- Protection
- Purification
- Spirituality

Colors

Choose colors that support your theme.

Black: protection
Blue: protection and change
Brown: earth
Gold: the gods, the sun, and solar deities
Indigo: change
Magenta: change
Orange: the sun

Purple: inspiration and spirituality
Red: life cycle
Silver: the goddesses
Violet: spiritual awareness
White: protection and purification

Colors for the Elements

Earth: black, brown, green, and gold
Air: white, lavender, and pale blue
Water: blue, blue-green, aquamarine, indigo, and white
Fire: red, orange, yellow, and gold

Crystals and Stones

Choose crystals and stones that support your theme.

Protection: agate, beryl, chrysoprase, citrine, jade, jasper, lapis lazuli, malachite, moonstone, obsidian, onyx, peridot, sapphire, sunstone, tiger's-eye, topaz, tourmaline, turquoise, and zircon

Protection and purification: garnet
Protection and spirituality: diamond lepidolite
Purification: aquamarine calcite
Spiritual transformation: alexandrite

Incense, Oils, and Herbs

Choose incense, oils, and herbs that support your theme.

Protection: agrimony, aloe, alyssum, amaranth, anemone, angelica, balm of Gilead, barley, basil, bittersweet, bladderwrack,

buckthorn, carnation, celandine, chrysanthemum, clover, cyclamen, dill, dragon's blood, elecampane, eucalyptus, fern, feverfew, geranium, ginseng, heather, holly, hyacinth, juniper, lady's slipper, mandrake, marjoram, violet, and wormwood

Purification: chamomile, copal, lemon verbena, and thyme

Purification and protection: bay, birch, bloodroot, broom, cedar, fennel, hyssop, lavender, parsley, sage, valerian, vervain, and yucca

Spirituality: cinnamon and gardenia

Spirituality and protection: African violet, frankincense, myrrh, and sandalwood

Altar Decorations

This is another ritual you won't get many chances to perform, so, again, feel free to make it as simple or as elaborate as you wish.

Using black and yellow or orange paper, you can cut out circles and glue them together to simulate the phases of a solar eclipse. These can be hung above your ritual area.

Use symbols to represent your other themes.

Incorporate the colors you have chosen with flowers, ribbons, and candles.

Make a fresh bouquet of your chosen herbs and flowers. Crush dried herbs and flowers into incense and burn on a charcoal tab. Pure oils can be dripped onto a lit charcoal tab to release a burst of scent in a beautiful cloud.

Ceremony

Begin your ritual as you normally would with your own version of creating a circle and calling the quarters. Once you have completed your normal ritual opening you may proceed using this sample ritual. You will also use your own closing once you have completed the specific ritual.

Say the following:

Mighty Lord, Father of us all, today your symbol, the sun, shall bid us a brief farewell as it disappears from sight. The eclipse should serve as a reminder to us all how deeply connected all life is to the sun. Our ancestors knew this, but today we take it for granted, it is something we forget. As the sun goes into hiding, we take this moment to honor the sun, to thank the sun for the life it gives us, for the warmth it gives us, for the light it gives us. Like our Lord, the sun dies but is still here for us, and will soon return. As the sun grows dark, we enter a time between times. It is both light and dark. It is both day and night. It is both, yet it is neither.

28

Meteor Shower

Themes

Choose two or three themes on which to center your ritual around.

- ✄ Celebrating life cycles
- ✄ The Elements
- ✄ The God
- ✄ The Goddess

- ✄ Protection
- ✄ Purification
- ✄ Spirituality

Colors

Choose colors that support your theme.

Black: protection
Blue: protection and change
Brown: earth
Gold: the gods, the sun, and solar deities
Indigo: change
Magenta: change
Orange: the sun
Purple: inspiration and spirituality

Red: life cycle
Silver: the goddesses
Violet: spiritual awareness
White: protection and purification

Colors for the Elements

Earth: black, brown, green, and gold
Air: white, lavender, and pale blue
Water: blue, blue-green, aquamarine, indigo, and white
Fire: red, orange, yellow, and gold

Crystals and Stones

Choose crystals and stones that support your theme.

Protection: agate, beryl, chrysoprase, citrine, jade, jasper, lapis lazuli, malachite, moonstone, obsidian, onyx, peridot, sapphire, sunstone, tiger's-eye, topaz, tourmaline, turquoise, and zircon
Protection and purification: garnet
Protection and spirituality: diamond lepidolite
Purification: aquamarine calcite
Spiritual transformation: alexandrite

Incense, Oils, and Herbs

Choose incense, oils, and herbs that support your theme.

Protection: agrimony, aloe, alyssum, amaranth, anemone, angelica, balm of Gilead, barley, basil, bittersweet, bladderwrack,

buckthorn, carnation, celandine, chrysanthemum, clover, cyclamen, dill, dragon's blood, elecampane, eucalyptus, fern, feverfew, geranium, ginseng, heather, holly, hyacinth, juniper, lady's slipper, mandrake, marjoram, violet, and wormwood

Purification: chamomile, copal, lemon verbena, and thyme

Purification and protection: bay, birch, bloodroot, broom, cedar, fennel, hyssop, lavender, parsley, sage, valerian, vervain, and yucca

Spirituality: cinnamon and gardenia

Spirituality and protection: African violet, frankincense, myrrh, and sandalwood

Altar Decorations

This can be a fun ritual to decorate for: cut out (or make) pictures of meteor showers, stars, planets, and hang them or place on the altar. You can find star-shaped confetti to scatter all over. Because it is easiest to see meteor showers at night, the decorations for this ritual should reflect the night sky.

Use symbols to represent your other chosen themes.

Incorporate the colors you have chosen with flowers, ribbons, and candles.

Make a fresh bouquet of your chosen herbs and flowers. Crush dried herbs and flowers into incense and burn on a charcoal tab. Pure oils can be dripped onto a lit charcoal tab to release a burst of scent in a beautiful cloud.

Ceremony

Begin your ritual as you normally would with your own version of creating a circle and calling the quarters. Once you have completed your normal ritual opening you may proceed using this sample ritual. You will also use your own closing once you have completed the specific ritual.

Say the following:

> *Mighty Lord and gentle Lady, tonight we watch as it appears the very stars are falling from the sky. Bright lights appear and shoot across the deep blue for a brief instance and then burn out, reminding us how short our lives on this Earth are. We must learn to make the most of this life while we are here, and to prepare ourselves for the next life we shall live.*

At this time, you can sit and watch the meteor shower, making sure to make a wish on a shooting star! Then repeat the above before closing the circle.

APPENDIX A

How to Write the Words to Your Rituals

When it comes to writing the words to rituals, many people are worried that they might not do it right. They are concerned about messing up or saying the wrong thing.

Unfortunately, there are some books out there that actually tell the reader that he or she must follow a set format, and the reader must do it exactly as the book dictates. This just isn't so.

The beauty of Paganism is that we can all follow our own paths and do what feels right for each of us. A ritual is basically a prayer to the deities, elements, and other beings; therefore, how and what you feel is not only appropriate, but also "right."

Whereas yes, a ritual is serious business, we need to get over the fear of saying the wrong thing. This is extremely true for solitary practitioners who need to write their own rituals. I know of no one who has been struck down by the God or Goddess because the right words weren't used in a ritual.

The wording to a ritual should come straight from your heart. You don't need to use fancy words, you don't need to rhyme every other line, and you don't have to have a degree in English to write a successful ritual.

To start your ritual writing, go over the different aspects of a ritual and figure out what your ritual is for and what purpose it is you want it to serve.

Next, sit back and relax. If you practice meditation, perhaps you would like to meditate on the purpose of your ritual. Keep pen and paper handy, and write down any thoughts that come to you during your meditation. Boost your creativity by using an oil such as bergamot. Bounce ideas off of friends—brainstorm.

There really is no right or wrong way to come up with your ritual. Someone else might not like your ritual, but you aren't writing it for someone else, you are writing it for yourself. You are writing it for your deities. You are writing it from your own experiences, from your own thoughts, from your own beliefs. If it feels right to you, it most likely *is* right for you.

APPENDIX B

Worksheet

 se this worksheet as a template to record your rituals in your Book of Shadows.

Ritual title: _____

Ritual purpose: _____

Themes: _____

Colors used: _____

Crystals and stones used: _____

Herbs, oils, and/or incense used: _____

Altar decorations: _____

Ceremony: _____

Participants: _____

Feast menu: _____

Special activities: _____

INDEX

Index

About the Author

Kerri Connor is also the author of *The Pocket Spell Creator: Magickal References at Your Fingertips*, *The Pocket Idiot's Guide to Potions*, and former editor of *The Circle of Stones Journal*.

Kerri is the High Priestess of the Sisterhood of Les Feys D'Avalon, and has been practicing her craft for 18 years.

She has been published in several magazines and newsletters including *The Blessed Bee*, *Sage Woman*, *PanGaia*, and *New Witch*. Currently, she runs the Website *The Pagan Review* (*www.thepaganreview.com*) on behalf of the Sisterhood.

A graduate from the University of Wisconsin, Kerri holds a B.A. in communications.

Kerri dances under the moon in rural Illinois. She loves reading, writing, gardening, and the Chicago Bears.